D1398855

THE GEORGIA REGIONAL LIBRARY FOR THE BLIND AND PHYSICALLY HANDICAPPED IS A FREE SERVICE FOR INDIVIDUALS UNABLE TO READ STANDARD PRINT.

ASK AT OUR CIRCULATION DESK HOW TO REGISTER FOR THIS SERVICE, AS WELL AS OTHER SERVICES OFFERED BY THIS LIBRARY.

Vengeance Rider

Vengeance Rider

Lewis Patten

THORNDIKE
CHIVERS

This Large Print edition is published by Thorndike Press®, Waterville, Maine USA and by BBC Audiobooks, Ltd, Bath, England.

Published in 2005 in the U.S. by arrangement with Golden West Literary Agency.

Published in 2005 in the U.K. by arrangement with Golden West Literary Agency.

U.S. Hardcover 0-7862-7597-9 (Western)
U.K. Hardcover 1-4056-3392-1 (Chivers Large Print)
U.K. Softcover 1-4056-3393-X (Camden Large Print)

The text of this Large Print edition is unabridged.
Other aspects of the book may vary from the original edition.

Set in 16 pt. Plantin by Elena Picard.

Printed in the United States on permanent paper.

British Library Cataloguing-in-Publication Data available

Library of Congress Cataloging-in-Publication Data

Patten, Lewis B.
    Vengeance rider / by Lewis Patten.
        p. cm. — (Thorndike Press large print Westerns)
    ISBN 0-7862-7597-9 (lg. print : hc : alk. paper)
    1. Married women — Crimes against — Fiction.
    2. Ex-convicts — Fiction. 3. Widowers — Fiction.
    4. Revenge — Fiction. 5. Large type books. I. Title.
    II. Thorndike Press large print Western series.
    PS3566.A79V46 2005
    813′.54—dc22   2005002913

Vengeance Rider

Chapter One

Ross Logan had thought about it many times — about this homecoming. Now he halted his horse atop Cheyenne Ridge, marking the southern boundary of the valley and stared into the haze-shrouded distance toward the town of Vail lying at its northern edge.

He couldn't see the town; it was hidden by distance and by a depression in the valley landscape. He couldn't see Horseshoe, the sprawling ranch that had once been home to him. But he knew the precise location of both. In some respects it was as though he had never been away at all.

A tall, lean man, he sat his horse with a practised ease that fifteen years had not been able to take from him. His face was angular, high-cheekboned and reddened by sun and wind. His mouth was firm, without softness in this moment. His eyes were brooding, filled with the anger that had smouldered in him these past fifteen years. His hair was streaked with grey and lines of bitterness were in his face. He was trouble for the valley of the Horseshoe. He was trouble and they'd know it as soon as they knew that he was back.

Somewhere in this valley there was a trail. It had grown cold over the passing years, but it was a trail he would find no matter how crooked, no matter how dim.

He shrugged lightly. The trail had waited fifteen years for him to return and explore it. It would wait a little longer. Right now he was hungry. He was tired and needed rest. They gave a man a ten dollar bill and a cheap suit of clothes when they opened the ponderous prison gates for him. The ten dollars would buy neither a horse nor very much in the way of food.

So he'd stayed in the prison town, working at whatever he could, for three long months. Eventually he'd earned enough money to buy a horse and a saddle some drifter had lost in a poker game. There hadn't been much left for food along the way. The last of the money had been spent two days ago. The last of the food had been gone for a day and a half.

He touched the horse's thin sides with his heels and it moved listlessly down the rocky slope toward the valley floor. Reaching it, the animal plodded patiently northward, angling east at Ross's direction toward Horseshoe Ranch.

The morning sun climbed across a cloudless sky and the still summer air turned hot. Unwillingly, nervousness touched Ross's thoughts.

Fifteen years was too long to be away. Everything would be changed. The little kids that had yelled and played in the streets of Vail during his trial would be grown men and women now. His father . . . A frown touched his face. His father would have aged. He might even have gone away.

But Phil Rivers, the only friend who had stuck by him during those difficult days . . . Phil would remember him. So would Tobias Vail, for whom the town had been named. Vail would remember him and would probably hate him still. Sadie Plue would remember him. Her five sons would be grown men now, steadied from the reckless youngsters they had been fifteen years ago.

He wondered if Juan Mascarenas was still sheriff. Juan had arrested him as he rode into the yard at Horseshoe. Juan had held him in jail during the trial and had accompanied him as he went to the prison in chains.

Orv Milburn would remember him too. Orv was probably a judge by now, but fifteen years ago he had been just starting out. He had defended Ross unsuccessfully at the trial.

There were others that he'd remember when he saw them on the streets. There were the women of the town, who had looked at him with pinched mouths and hate-filled eyes as though he were a threat to all their sex and had to be destroyed before his poison spread.

The strange part of it, he remembered, was that everyone in Horseshoe county had thought him guilty of killing Ruth — perhaps because they knew how much justification he had. Or because they didn't know. His mouth twisted bitterly.

Orv Milburn got him off with a second-degree murder conviction. There weren't any witnesses or even any proof. Orv convinced the jury that because of the way she was beaten it must have been done in a rage. He'd thought about that a lot since then. Orv's defence hadn't been much of a defence. At the time, Ross had thought he just didn't have the necessary experience. Now . . .

A grimace of distaste suddenly touched his face. It was over and he should be able to forget. Yet he knew that by coming back he was renewing everything. He would freshen the crime, not only in his own mind but in the minds of all the county's inhabitants.

The miles dragged along behind the horse's plodding hoofs. In mid-morning, he crossed a corner of land belonging to the Vail Land and Cattle Company and shortly crossed the boundary of Horseshoe Ranch itself. The cattle he saw now bore the familiar Horseshoe brand.

This ranch and all the cattle had been gobbled up by the expense of the trial. There had been a panic fifteen years ago. Cattle were selling for practically nothing and there was no market at all for land.

Orv Milburn handled the sale. Tom Logan, Ross's father, had been in St. Louis digging into Ruth's past and trying to find some evidence that would clear his son.

He'd been home, though, on the last day of the trial. Beaten, discouraged, he had sat in the rear of the courtroom staring at the floor.

It was puzzling to Ross that he had heard from his father only once in the entire fifteen years. That had been a month after Juan Mascarenas left him in the Warden's charge. But he knew his father was still alive. He'd have heard if his father had died.

At noon, he saw the ranch buildings of Horseshoe lying directly ahead of him, shimmering and distorted by rising waves of heat from the sun-baked land.

There was deterioration in the buildings, but there were a lot of new corrals — three times as many as there had been last time he saw the place. All were seven feet high and built of stout spruce poles.

Horse corrals, he thought. One, large and round, contained a bunch of about fifty horses.

He rode in at a plodding walk. The smell of frying meat drifted toward him from the house. It made the saliva begin to run in his mouth and made his stomach knot and cramp with pain.

A man was washing up at the pump a dozen feet from the back door. He glanced up, towelling his face.

He was a broad, thick brute of a man, shorter than Ross but weighing at least thirty pounds more. He appeared to be in his mid-fifties, and his head was growing bald.

His eyes were narrow, mere slits in his darkly weathered face, and were cold blue-grey. His mouth, also thin, was hard and turned down slightly at the corners. A stubble of greying whiskers covered his face.

Ross rode to him but did not dismount. He waited for the man's invitation to get down but it didn't come. At last Ross said angrily, trying not to glance toward the house from which those tantalising food smells came, "I could use a meal. I'll work for it."

The man's voice was a rasp. "After you've eaten it, I suppose. You goddam saddle tramps . . ."

A flush stained Ross's face. He said, "Before, if that's the way you want it."

The man studied him calculatingly for several moments. Then he gestured with his head toward the corral full of horses. "They're wild and need breakin'. A horse for a meal. If you want to eat, get at it."

Ross glanced around at this place where he'd spent so many of his years. He clenched his teeth. In the old days whoever rode in had been welcome to stay and eat. Or to stay the night.

But he needed a meal. More than that, he wanted to stay here for a while if he could. It was home to him. It was where Ruth had died and because it was, the trail he had to find began right here.

He nodded shortly and rode across the yard to the corral. He dismounted, took a rope off one of the protruding poles and opened the gate.

His head whirled, both from hunger and the heat. It had been fifteen years since he'd had a rope in his hands, since he'd topped off a wild one, but he didn't suppose a man forgot. He made a loop and it sailed out over the heads of the milling broncs.

It missed and he coiled it again. On his second throw, the loop settled over the head of a chunky steel-grey.

He snatched a hackamore from a nail, moved to the centre of the corral and snubbed the grey. The animal fought furiously for several minutes before it stood, trembling and covered with sweat.

Ross didn't look around to see if the blocky man was watching him. He could feel a wild, irrational anger rising in his mind.

He fought the horse several more moments before he got the hackamore on. He was shaking violently as he crossed the corral and got a saddle from the top pole of the corral.

More minutes were consumed in getting it cinched down. His knees weak and trembling, he put a foot into the stirrup and swung astride.

The horse exploded under him. He stayed for two jumps and went sailing off on the third.

He didn't glance toward the gate, but he heard the thick man's bellow of laughter.

Furiously he got to his feet. His body had its limitations but his determination did not. He stumbled across the corral and caught the horse again.

This time he waited several moments until his breathing quieted, until the tremors in his knees diminished. Then he mounted the horse a second time.

Anger gave him strength he had not possessed before. He stuck stubbornly to the horse's back while the animal pitched violently back and forth across the crowded corral.

Twice he slammed against the poles. Both times Ross barely got his leg up in time to keep it from being crushed.

The body-jolting punishment went on and on. It seemed to be continuing forever. The world became a reeling blur to him in which there was only one burning purpose — to stay on this damned grey's back until he quit.

The horse did quit — so suddenly that Ross nearly fell out of the saddle from surprise. His nose was bleeding and he swiped at it with the back of his hand. He rode the horse around the corral for two full circles before he slid off exhaustedly at the gate. He removed the saddle, dropped it on the ground, then removed the hackamore and turned the grey loose. His head whirling, he leaned wearily against the gate a moment before he hung up the hackamore and heaved the saddle back to the top pole where it had been before.

He opened the gate and stumbled out. He stared at the thick-set owner of the place. He said hoarsely, "Now let's eat."

"What's your name, mister?"

"Logan. Ross Logan."

The man scowled, studying him closely. Then he laughed shortly. "The wife-killer? The one who used to own this place? I thought you were down at the pen."

Ross's eyes burned but he didn't reply.

The man said flatly, "You get out of here. Get the hell out. I don't want any goddam killers on my place."

Ross said coldly, "That meal. I earned it and I want it."

The man seemed to be enjoying himself. "You get nothin'. You didn't tell me what you were."

Ross took a step toward him. He said softly, "One more time. Let's go eat."

There was deliberate cruelty in the man's eyes as he shook his head.

Ross swung with every bit of the strength that was left in him. His fist sank into the man's hard belly, driving a grunt from him. Ross swung again, at his jaw, and missed.

The man's fist struck him on the side of the head with force enough to slam him against the corral. He slid down the poles to the ground.

He shook his head and pulled himself to his feet. He staggered toward the man, only to be dropped again by a cruelly cutting, deliberate blow that landed squarely on his mouth.

He stayed down longer this time, tasting blood, but he made it up finally and approached the man unsteadily.

Something hot and lusting was in the thick-set man's tiny, slitted eyes. He slammed Ross back against the corral again, but this time he followed.

None of his blows were hard enough to knock Ross out. But each one hurt, or cut, or bruised. The man beat him deliberately until in the aggregate his blows robbed Ross of consciousness. Blackness descended over his mind and he did not even taste the dust into which his face slid. He lay unmoving, as though dead.

Chapter Two

The first thing he felt was something cold and wet dabbed gently against his bleeding face. He opened his eyes.

He was still lying on the ground immediately in front of the corral. But now he was on his back.

His face burned and his throat was dry. His vision blurred but there was no mistaking the fact that a woman's face was near to his, that a woman's hands were dabbing his face with a wet cloth.

He struggled to sit up, waited there until his head cleared, then got to his feet with the woman helping him. He asked, "Where is he?"

Her voice was throaty and soft. "He's gone to town."

"Who are you, his daughter?"

Her face coloured. "I'm Lily Caine. His wife."

Ross didn't reply. He stared at her.

She was at least twenty-five years younger

than her husband. He guessed she was in her mid-twenties. A pretty woman too. Her body was strong and well-shaped. Her hair was neat and shone from much brushing.

But her face, still holding its flush of embarrassment, was lifeless. She didn't look at Ross again, but kept her eyes downcast. Hers was an attractive face, or would be if it ever softened up, he thought. Her chin was firm beneath a mouth that was full and which had retained a certain sweetness even though it had apparently forgotten how to smile. Her lashes were long, her eyes large. Ross had gotten an impression that they were brown, but now he wasn't sure. Her brows were thick, her forehead high and smooth. Her cheeks seemed hollow beneath finely shaped cheekbones.

Her husband had taught her fear, Ross thought. She kept glancing uneasily in the direction of town.

She asked softly, "Do you think that you could eat?"

Ross nodded. He stumbled toward the pump and she followed, half a dozen steps behind.

She worked the pump handle and Ross stuck his head under the spout. The cold water stung his face where it had been cut. He scrubbed off the dust and blood and

19

took the towel she handed him. After that he followed her to the house.

He sank into a chair at the table and she began to fill a plate for him. When she brought it, he stared down at it ravenously. He would have to eat slowly, he thought, or afterward he'd lose everything he'd eaten.

He chewed deliberately and slowly, refusing more when Lily Caine offered it. He finished the coffee, though it burned his cut lips cruelly. He got up. "Thank you, Mrs. Caine."

She nodded acknowledgment but did not meet his eyes. He went out, crossed the yard to the pump and got himself a drink. He felt sick at his stomach from the food.

Lily Caine came out, carrying two buckets. Ross worked the pump handle for her. She glanced up at him, as though surprised, but she didn't speak. She started to pick up the buckets but Ross picked them up instead. He carried them to the house.

She followed, without looking directly at him once, and he went back outside.

Ross walked across the yard to his horse. He couldn't help thinking of Caine.

There had been intentional cruelty in the man as he beat Ross with his fists. It had never been a fight. There hadn't been enough strength in Ross to put up a decent fight.

He wondered what it was like for her being married to such a man. He shook his head bewilderedly.

Why did a woman marry a man like that? Caine might own Horseshoe, but from the looks of things he hung on to every dollar as though it would be the last he'd ever see. So if she married him for money she hadn't got what she bargained for.

He knew he ought to leave, but he couldn't bring himself to mount his horse. He knew that if he was going to retain what he had eaten, he had better remain still for a while.

He sat down, putting his back to the corral. His face hurt where Caine's fists had beaten it, and his body ached.

He knew his chances of finding Ruth's killer after fifteen years were poor. He also realised that finding him would neither restore the fifteen years he had lost, nor the ranch that had been sold to pay for his defence. Yet the smouldering anger of fifteen years was not to be denied. There was but one thing left in his life — to find the man for whose crime he had paid so heavily. And by finding him, prove those who had condemned him wrong.

He saw Caine coming and got to his feet. He leaned against the corral fence, watching. There was a short length of pole lying not far away. Caine wasn't going to beat him into unconsciousness again.

Caine rode directly to the corral. The ugly light was still in his eyes, but now something else was there as well. Obscure anger, unwillingness, and resentment too. He asked surlily, "Get your meal?"

Ross nodded, puzzlement touching him.

"Soreheaded about the beating? Or do you still want to stay?"

Ross said unbelievingly, "I'm soreheaded, but I want to stay."

"All right, stay then. I got plenty of horses to be broke and more coming. Pay's twenty a month an' keep. Sleep in the bunkhouse over there."

Ross asked suspiciously, "Why the change of heart?"

Caine scowled. Then he mumbled unconvincingly, "Well hell . . . a bitch like that . . . maybe anybody'd kill a bitch like that."

Ross led his horse to the barn. He put him into a stall and gave him a feed of hay. Afterward he crossed the yard to the bunkhouse. He didn't believe Caine's explanation of his change of heart. It was too lame, too weak, after his positive, violent attitude earlier.

He collapsed on one of the bunks. He was exhausted, but he didn't go to sleep immediately. His mind kept seeing Ruth, and he lived again his torment and disbelief as he came to know what she was. He remembered the soul-searching as he sought the cause, believing that somehow he had failed Ruth before she failed him. Patience and understanding had not been easy and he had not managed them too well. But he'd tried. Oh God, he'd tried . . .

He fell asleep, and dreamed that he was pursuing the killer of his wife. The man was too far ahead of him to be recognised and he could not catch up.

He awoke near sundown, got up and went out into the yard. He walked to the pump, worked the handle several times, then stuck his head under the spout.

He was hungry, and still stiff, both from the ride and the beating he had taken. But after supper he meant to ride into town. He had waited fifteen years and would wait no more.

The town looked no different to him than it had a hundred times before. In

23

early evening lights shone through the windows and open doors of the saloons. There were lights in the windows of the houses on both sides of Main. There was leisurely traffic along the street, a few buggies and buckboards, several horsemen . . .

He wondered if his father was here in town, and was not surprised that he felt little toward him any more. His father had only written him once in fifteen years. He supposed his father believed he was guilty just like everybody else. Perhaps he hadn't at first, but it was the only thing that could explain his later indifference.

He rode up Main and the feeling hit him almost immediately, so strongly it was like a smell in the still night air.

Hostility. Fear. They knew Ross Logan was back. They waited for his coming and wondered what he was going to do. Or was he just imagining it?

Up the exact centre of the street he rode, past the huge yellow livery barn, past the scattering of shops at the lower end of the street.

Someone was sitting on the bench in front of the jail, but Ross didn't stop until Juan Mascarenas's voice came softly through the darkness, "Ross."

He turned his horse toward the voice

and drew rein at the edge of the walk. Juan said, "Good to see you, Ross."

Ross said coldly, "Let's start out by saying what we mean. You're not glad to see me and I'm not glad to see you. But there's not much you can do about me. I paid for what I was supposed to have done. I'm a free man."

"You sound mighty bitter, Ross."

"Wouldn't you be bitter after spending fifteen years in the pen for something you didn't do? Do you know what it's like down there?"

"Why did you come back?"

"To do what you should have done fifteen years ago — find the man who really killed my wife."

Mascarenas puffed silently on his long cigar for several moments. Ross couldn't see his face, but he knew it would look a lot older than it had before. There would be grey in Juan's hair, new lines in his face. He could see that the sheriff's body was thicker, heavier than it had been at the trial.

Mascarenas asked, "Got a place to stay?"

"You know I have. I'm out at Horse-shoe."

"Breaking horses for meals?"

"Then you did talk to Caine?"

"I talked to him."

"Who else talked to him? Who'd he come in to see?"

"Ross, why don't you forget it and ride out of here? You're looking for trouble and if you stir that old fire up, you're liable to end up right back in the pen."

Ross peered at him, trying to see his face in the semidarkness. He said, "I can find out who he came in to see. Somebody else will tell me even if you don't."

Mascarenas muttered reluctantly, "He went to see the judge. Orv Milburn."

"Now why would he do that? Why would Orv be so interested in knowing I was back?"

The sheriff shrugged eloquently. "Maybe you give yourself too much importance, Ross. Maybe they talked about something else."

"What else would it be? A judge isn't supposed to handle legal matters for anyone, is he?"

Mascarenas didn't answer that. He asked, "Buy you a beer?"

"All right." Ross swung off his horse. He looped the reins around the rail. "Pa still around?"

"He's around."

"He all right?"

"Sure. Older. But we all are."

26

Mascarenas rose and Ross walked along the broadwalk with him toward the Antlers Saloon, half a dozen doors up the street. He asked, "How about Vail?"

"He's here."

"There's something I want to know about him, now that I'm back. I want to know why he suddenly started hating my guts right after you arrested me."

"He didn't hate you, Ross. Any more than . . ." The sheriff stopped and Ross finished the sentence bitterly, ". . . any more than anyone hates a wife-killer? Is that what you were going to say?"

"Ross, for God's sake . . ." Mascarenas paused helplessly. "It's all over, Ross. Stirring things up isn't going to give you back your fifteen years. Neither will it give you back your ranch. Let me get a stake together for you. Take it and go someplace where you aren't known. Pay it back when you can."

"Who'd contribute to that stake? Orv Milburn? Vail, maybe? You?"

"We were all your friends, Ross. Whether you believe it or not. What's wrong with giving you a hand?"

"I don't know, Juan. Maybe nothing. But I've got a feeling it's a payoff for going away and letting what's dead stay that way."

"Is that so bad?"

"It wouldn't be if I'd done what they sent me to the pen for."

Mascarenas murmured wearily, "Never was a man convicted who didn't swear he was innocent."

Ross didn't reply. Mascarenas held back at the doors of the Antlers and let him enter first.

He pushed on through. The place had changed. The bar was on the opposite side of the room from where it had been before. The walls had been painted at least once. The tables and chairs were new. A man was tending bar that Ross didn't even know.

But he knew several of the men at the bar. He knew Tobias Vail. And he knew Orv Milburn, Judge Milburn now.

Mascarenas grasped him lightly by the elbow. "The beer first, Ross."

He walked to the bar and the sheriff came up beside him. Mascarenas said, "Beer, Lou. A couple of them."

The bartender drew them and slid them expertly along the bar. Juan laid down a silver dollar.

Ross sipped the beer. It was good after all these years. He glanced aside at Vail and caught the man watching him, unconcealed hostility in his eyes. Ross stared back steadily until Vail looked away.

Milburn came around from the other end of the bar. "Heard you were back, Ross. Glad to see you again." He put out a hand that was soft in Ross's hard grasp. He was smiling affably, older now and growing heavy with the years. His head, exposed by his pushed-back black hat, was balding and pink.

Ross said, "Heard about it from Caine, huh? Now why did he run to you so fast when he found out who I was?"

Affability became strained in the judge's face. "Caine had to see me on another matter. He'd planned to come in to-day."

He put a hand on Ross's shoulder and gripped it. "We're your friends, Ross, remember that. What happened fifteen years ago is over and forgotten. I . . ."

Ross interrupted evenly, "It's over, but it isn't forgotten, Judge. I won't forget it until I turn the killer up."

Milburn clucked like a hen. "Your story hasn't changed, has it, Ross? I'd hoped . . ."

Ross said, "You think I was guilty, huh? Did you think so when you were defending me?"

"What a lawyer thinks . . ." Milburn paused helplessly. Then he said briskly, "Come up to my office tomorrow, Ross.

There are a few things to settle up. There were cattle found after you had gone. There were some old debts paid. I've been giving your father enough to live on, but some of it is left. Some money is coming to you."

"How much?"

"I don't recall offhand." Milburn frowned. "Over three hundred dollars, I think." He finished his drink and extended his hand again. This time, Ross just looked at it and after a moment it was withdrawn. Milburn's face flushed with confusion and embarrassment. He said lamely, "I just wish you didn't feel this way, Ross. I defended you."

Ross didn't reply. He kept his glance steadily on Milburn's face until the man turned away.

He returned his attention to his beer. Juan Mascarenas asked softly, "What the hell are you trying to do? See how many enemies you can make?"

Ross shook his head. "I'm just trying to find out who my enemies really are." If he'd known about the three hundred dollars Milburn said was coming to him, he could have saved himself three months of working down at the pen after his release. He could have started home three months earlier.

Chapter Three

An impression stayed with Ross, vague and unsubstantiated, but in which he believed at least. It was an impression that Milburn had lied to him.

Whether he had lied about Caine's visit or about the money or both, Ross didn't know. But he was sure his impression was correct.

Why should Milburn lie? Was it possible he had killed Ruth or knew who had? Ross shook his head almost imperceptibly. Milburn hadn't even known Ruth so far as he knew. It was possible, of course, that Milburn knew who the real killer was. But it was doubtful. There would be no advantage to him in concealing such knowledge. On the contrary it seemed to Ross that a judge, who depended upon votes, could get a lot of valuable publicity by turning up the real killer even after all this time.

Another reason then. But what reason

could there be? Could Milburn have lined his own pockets out of the sale of Horseshoe Ranch?

That possibility made more sense. Ross put the thought in the back of his mind for later examination. A lot of toes, including Milburn's, would probably get stepped on before he was through.

He turned his head and stared at Vail. The man had aged considerably in the past fifteen years. He must be close to sixty now, Ross thought. He would have been forty-five at the time of Ruth's death.

Ross had always gotten along all right with Vail — before Ruth's death at least. Why, then, had Vail's attitude toward him changed afterward?

The intensity of his glance drew Vail's. The man turned his head.

His eyes were cold blue — as cold as the sky on a winter day or the ice in a mountain stream. His face was lined, but it was still firm and his skin was like leather. His mouth, beneath a white, cavalry-style moustache, was thin and hard. He said harshly, "Stay clear of me, Logan. Stay clear of me and stay off my land. I don't like you any better now than I did fifteen years ago."

"Why?"

"You're a killer, that's why, an' a woman-killer to boot. She was worth ten of the likes of you."

"I didn't know you knew her well enough to decide that."

"I knew her well enough. All a man had to do was look at her . . ." Angrily he poured himself another drink. He downed it at a gulp, turned and strode from the saloon without looking at Ross again.

Ross frowned. Ruth had looked like an angel, he remembered. She had been the most beautiful woman he had ever seen. He wondered suddenly if that very beauty might not have been behind the things she did. Because of it, every man who ever saw her wanted her. And if she had been as uncertain inside as most people were . . . she had needed admiration.

But why had she needed it from every man she met? And why hadn't she been satisfied with admiration, which men gave her readily? He shook his head almost angrily. It hadn't mattered who rode in at the ranch . . . as long as he was away . . .

The memory made a kind of nausea stir in his stomach. Juan Mascarenas said, "Beer make you sick? Maybe you ought to have coffee or something."

Ross shook his head. He asked, "What

happens if you find the real killer after all these years?"

Juan stared at him warily. "If it happened, we'd prosecute him. He'd go to the pen."

"And what about me?"

Juan shrugged. "Sometimes the state legislature makes restitution for false imprisonment. It's happened. But they have to pass a special bill and it doesn't very often get done."

Ross turned. He said, "Thanks for the beer, Sheriff."

"Sure, Ross." He was silent a moment, but when Ross started away, he said, "Ross, let it drop. Even if you didn't do it, like you say, it'd be better all around if you let it drop."

Ross stared at him steadily. "Sheriff, I don't think they're going to let me drop it. And if they would, do you want a killer running loose?"

Mascarenas didn't reply. Ross could see he wasn't even seriously considering the possibility that an unknown killer was running loose. He thought Ross had done it. He firmly believed that now even if he hadn't fifteen years ago.

He asked, "Where does my father live?"

"You remember the old shack where Phil

Running-Horse used to live?"

Ross nodded.

"He lives in that."

Ross turned away quickly and went outside. From Horseshoe Ranch to Phil Running-Horse's shack was quite a come-down for his father — something else Horseshoe County had to answer for.

He walked down the street toward his horse, which he had tied in front of the jail. Something about Vail kept bothering him. He supposed Vail could have begun hating him simply because he believed him guilty of killing Ruth. Even if he hadn't known her very well. If he had known her well — as well as Ross, for example — he might have felt differently.

Ross's face twisted in the darkness. He might have left Ruth long before her death, save for one thing. Her remorse over her own actions. Her tears and her prom-ises . . .

He put his thoughts of Ruth away from him violently. He put thoughts of Vail and Orv Milburn in the back of his mind, for further consideration when he was not so tired, when his brain would be functioning better than it was now.

He reached his horse, unwound the reins and swung stiffly to the saddle. He turned the animal and headed down the street toward Phil Running-Horse's shack.

The night air was soft and cool. On such a night, he remembered unwillingly, he had married Ruth. They had driven in this same direction out to Horseshoe Ranch, excited and breathless with the realisation of what lay ahead of them.

He tried to stop thinking and failed. The memory of her was like a pain in his chest where still, after fifteen years, lived the hurt, the disillusionment and despair. But it hadn't been like that at first. And he'd refused to believe his own suspicions for a long, long time.

He'd met her in Kansas City where he'd gone with a trainload of steers. He'd wanted her — like every man who ever saw her.

He shook his head angrily. Maybe Juan Mascarenas was right. Maybe coming back had been a big mistake. His memories were too painful and returning had only freshened and stirred them up.

The shack sat by itself surrounded by vacant lots just short of the place where First Street crossed Main. It loomed clearly against the lighter background of uncut weeds.

It had been dilapidated fifteen years ago.

Now it was worse. Even in darkness Ross could see places where the shingles were gone from the roof, and could see the rusty tin patches that had been put over the holes. The porch sagged as though it might fall down if someone stepped on it. There was a broken window on the side from which Ross approached.

Short of the shack by twenty feet, Ross's horse suddenly shied. Glancing down, he saw a man's body lying in the dust.

He dismounted immediately. The man was snoring softly. He reeked of alcohol, but there was an unwashed smell about him too. His clothes were ragged and dirty. He had a week's growth of greyish whiskers on his face.

It was an instant before Ross recognised him. The change had been too great. But it was his father. It was his father, passed out here in the dusty street.

A wave of hatred flowed through Ross's mind — hatred for the town, the county, the people who had done this to a man who had once been strong and proud. They had wrecked more than one life when they convicted him of killing Ruth. They had broken his father, had made a drunken wreck of him. It explained why Ross hadn't heard from his father all these years.

And Milburn — supplying money from what he said was recovered cattle and collected debts — had made the continuation of Tom Logan's drunkenness a virtual certainty.

He stopped, slid his arms beneath his father's arms and raised him up, startled at his father's lack of weight. The old man grunted protestingly a couple of times, but did not come to.

Ross carried him into the house. His foot encountered an empty tin can on the floor and it clattered against the wall. He could hear mice scurrying to safety.

He laid his father down on the bed. He fumbled for a match, struck it and stared around, looking for the lamp.

Finding it, he lighted it and trimmed the wick. The chimney was black with soot and the lamp gave off very little light. But there was enough to see the untidy condition of the room. There was enough to see the squalor in which his father lived.

His eyes burned with a growing anger that was, for the moment at least, helpless. This would change. A lot of things would change. But it was going to take time.

He'd accept the three hundred from Milburn. It would help, whether it was what Milburn said it was or not. He'd get this place cleaned up and his father so-bered. Somehow, somewhere, he'd find the beginning of the killer's trail. And finding that, perhaps he'd find some other answers too.

He stared around the single room again. There wasn't a thing he could do here to-night. It would take his father six or eight hours, maybe more, to sleep this one off.

He straightened out his father's uncon-scious body on the bed. He covered him, grimacing with distaste at the condition of the blanket. He crossed the room and blew out the lamp. He went out and closed the door behind.

His horse still stood where he had left him a short distance away. He walked to him and mounted, then turned down the street again.

He was suddenly glad that he had come back. His anger, his bitterness, his hunger for revenge were stronger to-night than they had ever been before.

Someone had to pay for his fifteen years in the pen. But more than that, they had to pay for the destruction of Tom Logan.

And someone would pay. Ross wouldn't rest until they had.

Chapter Four

He awakened as dawn's first grey light filtered through the dirty bunkhouse windows, sat on the edge of the bunk and rubbed his eyes. He stood up, yawned luxuriously, then pulled on his pants. He slipped into his shirt, then sat down again and pulled on his boots.

His body ached cruelly, both from the bronc ride yesterday and the beating Caine had given him. He put on his hat and went outside.

Smoke was issuing from the kitchen chimney. Caine was at the pump, washing up. The horses milled around in the corral, squealing and kicking at each other.

Ross crossed the yard and stared through the poles at them. He hated the thought of working all day for Caine, using time that might be spent looking for the things he had to find. Yet he knew that time was of little importance now. He was back. He wasn't going to find the trail he sought to-day, or to-morrow, or maybe even this month. It was going to take a lot of time.

But if he worked steadily here, his very inactivity might make someone in the county uncomfortable. The man he was hunting might make the first move out of nervousness.

Furthermore, staying here would give him time to think, and to build up his strength, sapped from heat, poor food, the backbreaking prison work and the long ride home.

He shook out a loop, entered the corral and roped a horse. He snubbed the animal to the post in the middle of the corral and watched dispassionately as the animal fought the rope. He heard Caine's harsh voice, "You start early, don't you?"

"I'll let him get used to the rope while we're eating breakfast. Afterward I'll give him a ride."

He half-hitched the rope and walked to the corral gate. He went out, turning his head as he did to look at the trembling horse.

He walked toward the pump, with Caine keeping pace beside him. He asked, "How long have you had this place?"

Caine's eyes narrowed. He glanced aside at Ross. "Long time. Why?"

"I just wondered. Whoever bought it from us got it mighty cheap."

"That wasn't me. I came here ten-twelve years ago." There was something wary and suspicious in Caine's harsh voice. Ross frowned inwardly, wondering what Caine was trying to hide.

He asked suddenly, "How long has my father been a drunk?"

"Long as I've been here." There seemed to be a certain relief in Caine that the subject had been changed.

Fifteen years. For that long a time Orv Milburn had been doling out money to Tom Logan, money he now claimed had come from the sale of strays and from uncollected debts. But had it come from that? Tom Logan had to eat as well as drink. It would take a lot of money to keep him in both food and liquor for fifteen years. Orv even claimed that over three hundred dollars was still left.

He washed at the pump. Caine went inside. When Ross had finished, he followed him.

Lily Caine had her back to him. She was standing at the stove. This morning he could not help notice how finely her back was made, how straight she held her shoulders. She turned, and for an instant, her glance met his.

It was lowered immediately, but not before something intangible passed between them. Puzzled at himself, Ross pulled out a chair and sat down.

The look had been short, but Caine hadn't missed it. He was staring at Ross and the cruelty had returned to his eyes. He said, "She ain't worth what I'll do to you if you put a hand on her."

Ross could feel his face growing hot. It angered him because there had been nothing improper in his thoughts about Lily Caine. He promised himself that before he left Horseshoe he would finish what Caine himself had begun yesterday.

Caine laughed mockingly. "She ain't much anyhow. She ain't pretty and she ain't smart. She's lazy besides."

Ross glanced up and met his eyes. Caine laughed again. "Must be somethin' about this place that makes the women here want every man that comes along. They tell me your wife was like that . . ."

Ross said flatly, "Shut up."

"You mean you're still touchy about it after all these years? She must've been somethin', that wife of yours."

Ross stood up. He said, "I told you to shut up."

Caine's tone was immediately conciliatory. "Don't get all riled up, Logan. Sit down and eat."

Ross sat down reluctantly. Lily Caine came up behind him and put a plate in front of him. He began to eat.

She went around to her husband and served him too. She did not sit down herself.

Ross ate swiftly, his eyes fixed on his plate. When he had finished he got up and strode outside.

He was beginning to understand Caine. There was deliberate cruelty in him that made him want to hurt people. The talk in the kitchen a few moments ago must have cut Lily like a knife. Caine had discussed her with him as though she had been an animal.

And yet, when the object of his cruelty fought back, Caine retreated every time. And waited for another opportunity when his victim's guard was down . . .

Angrily, he went into the corral. He put a hackamore on the horse he had snubbed to the post, saddled and swung astride. Ten minutes later, the horse quit and Ross slid to the ground. Caine was standing at the gate watching him. He had a horse saddled and was holding the reins.

"I'm going over to the badlands and see Sadie Plue. She's supposed to have a new bunch of broncs for me."

Ross walked to the gate. "How do you have time for cattle if you spend all your time breaking broncs?"

"Don't take much time for cattle this time of year." Caine's eyes were oddly wary. He mounted his horse, stared at Ross for a moment, then turned and rode away.

Ross watched him. Caine was half a mile away before he turned.

Lily Caine was hanging out clothes on a line strung between the house and a small tree nearby. She didn't look at him, but he had the feeling she had been watching him until he turned.

Impatiently he crossed the corral, shook out a loop and roped another horse. He snubbed him to the post.

He fought horses until noon, his mind half on the horses and half on the problem he faced. At noon, Lily Caine crossed the yard and called to him. "Mr. Logan. Dinner is ready."

She ducked her head when he turned and looked at her. Frowning, he released the horse he had been working with and came out of the corral.

Having washed at the pump, he went to the house. Caine had not yet returned.

He sat down at the table and watched her openly as she worked. A slight flush crept into her cheeks.

She served him and returned to the stove. He said, "Come set down."

She seemed about to protest, but then abruptly did as he requested. She met his glance briefly, almost defiantly.

He stared at her. "Why did you marry him?" he asked bluntly.

Her cheeks pink, she glanced up and met his gaze again. "You have no right to ask me that."

"I suppose I haven't, but I'm asking anyway. He's got more consideration for the horse he rides than he has for you."

"He's my husband."

"Sure he is!" Sudden, obscure anger touched him. He wanted to force her to show some emotion, even if it was only anger. "And are you satisfied with the bargain you made? Has he got enough money to make it worth your while?"

Her eyes did not evade his now. They flashed at him furiously. "I didn't marry him for money! I . . ." Those angry eyes suddenly filled with tears. Ross put out a hand involuntarily and covered hers, but she withdrew it as though his touch had burned. Still angry, she said, "How could you know what it was like? I was only seventeen. We were travelling through here on our way to California when my mother and father both took sick. They died within a week and everything we had went to bury them. I tried to get a job but there were no jobs — except the kind I wouldn't take. And Mr. Caine was kind to me . . ."

"So you married him."

"Yes."

"You could have left him when you found out what he was really like."

Now her glance met his very steadily. "Yes, I could, couldn't I? It's always easy to quit."

Ross said softly, "I'm sorry." He picked up the pot of stew from the centre of the table and passed it to her. He watched her face as he said, "He says you're not pretty, but you are."

"You shouldn't say such things to me." She lowered her glance to her plate.

"Someone should."

"Why?" The word was scarcely audible.

"Because they make you feel good. And because they're true."

She glanced at him gratefully. There was obvious vulnerability apparent in her eyes, and a certain helplessness. She was hungry for the tenderness that women need, starving for the love all humans need.

Ross had been long without a woman and suddenly the need for her was almost overpowering. He felt his muscles tense.

He jumped to his feet, leaving his meal unfinished, and strode angrily outside. He tramped across the yard to the corral.

He was not proud of the things he had been thinking back there. He had been thinking that everything that made life worthwhile had been unjustly taken from him. He had been asking himself why he should not now take the things he wanted, no matter who it hurt.

Caine himself had planted the idea in his mind. But with Lily . . . she was as vulnerable as a girl. She had been so long without kindness, without consideration or love that she had no defence against it.

He turned his head and stared back at the house. Then, purposefully, he strode to the barn where he bridled and saddled his horse. He rode out of the barn and took the road to town without looking back.

He knew he shouldn't stay at Horseshoe now. He told himself that he hadn't known Lily Caine long enough to be in love with her. He needed a woman, but any woman would do. He didn't need someone else's wife. He didn't need Lily Caine.

But all the way to town her face remained in his thoughts. He couldn't erase that last, long look she had given him.

A trusting look, but a startled and surprised one too. He clenched his teeth angrily.

He rode in at the foot of Main and went directly to his father's shack. He knocked, then opened the door and went inside.

Tom Logan was sitting on the side of the rumpled bunk, his eyes red, his hair tousled. He looked up without immediate recognition.

Ross said, "Hello, Pa. It's me, Ross."

Tom Logan rubbed his eyes. He stood up, self-consciously smoothing his clothes. He ran a hand through his tousled hair. He started to speak, then looked at the floor. When he glanced up again there was open defiance in his eyes. "Well, how do you like what you see? We're a pair, ain't we? A jailbird and a drunk."

For a moment Ross was silent. Then he said, "It doesn't have to be that way. I didn't kill Ruth. I've done nothing that I have to spend my life apologising for. And you don't have to apologise for me."

The old man stared at him. He mum-

49

bled, "Why'd you have to come back anyway?"

Ross's eyes burned. "I came back here because this is the only home I know. I came back to collect a debt."

"What debt? Nobody owes us anything."

"You're wrong. Somebody owes me for the fifteen years I spent in the pen. Somebody owes us for Horseshoe. I intend to collect."

His father sat down limply on the bunk and stared up at him. He said wearily, "You're talking about revenge. You're talking about something that will put you right back in the pen. Or on the gallows."

"Maybe. But this time it will be for something I did, not for something I didn't do."

Tom Logan muttered almost angrily, "I need a drink. I can't think straight."

"All right. Come on and we'll both have one. One. Then we'll come back here and you'll get yourself cleaned up. We'll clean up this shack."

He stared down at his father. Fifteen years of hiding in a bottle had all but erased what Ross remembered about him. Before he had been sent away, his father had been strong, capable, unafraid. Why had Ross's conviction done so much damage to him?

A terrible thought intruded into his mind. Could it be? He shook his head almost angrily. But this was something he had to know, and now. He said, "Let's talk about Ruth for a minute before we go. You knew what she was like even before I did, didn't you?"

Tom Logan's face twisted almost involuntarily with pain. He nodded numbly.

"Was there . . . ? Did she ever make a try for you?"

Logan looked up, his face contorted. He tried to meet Ross's glance and failed. At last he nodded miserably.

Ross's chest began to hurt. He waited.

The old man looked up. "I never touched her. I swear to God! She tried to get me to, but I didn't. I don't know who killed her. I thought you had. If somebody hadn't beat me to it I'd probably have killed her myself. Because she made me want her! My own son's wife! And when they sent you to prison because they thought you'd done what I'd ought to have done myself . . . !"

Ross's whole body felt limp, wrung out. He stared down at his father's bowed head. Tom Logan had paid more heavily than he over the past fifteen years. He had paid with guilt that ate at his mind like a sore. To drown it he drank. Until there was only this left of him.

Ross's voice was soft. "It's out now, Pa. It's out and it doesn't have to eat at you any more. I know what she was like."

Tom Logan put his face down into his hands. His body shook. Ross put a hand on his shoulder and gripped it. It was thin, scarcely more than skin and bones.

He'd known what Ruth was like all right, but not until the last few months before her death. Once he'd beaten a man insensible that he'd found with her — because she claimed she was forced. He discovered that his hands were clenched. The truth comes hard . . . but he'd admitted the truth at last . . .

He stared at the broken body of his father. Fury made his skin burn. Time was now something he no longer had plenty of. Patience was gone from him.

He said harshly, "Come on, Pa. We'll get you a drink to steady you. Then we'll go to work."

Tom Logan glanced up. There was moisture in his reddened eyes. "I don't know . . . it's been so long. I don't even know if I *can* quit drinking now."

"You can quit. Because I need your help."

Chapter Five

The sun was blinding as the pair stepped out into the street. Tom Logan shuffled along beside Ross, making a valiant effort to hold up his head, to throw his shoulders back. They passed the jail without seeing Juan Mascarenas and went on to the Antlers. A few steps short of the door, Tom Logan caught Ross's arm. "No, I don't want a drink. If I have one then I'll have to have another."

Ross turned his head. His father had been almost as tall as he when he went away. The old man seemed to have shrunk because now he had to look down at him.

He said, "Then hit the barbershop. Get a bath and a shave. I'll go see Orv Milburn and come back for you."

His father stared up at him for several moments. His eyes were watering but it might have been from the glare of the sun. He said hoarsely, "Ross, I'm glad you're back."

Ross nodded shortly and watched him cross the street toward the barbershop. Mascarenas had also said he was glad Ross was back, as had Orv Milburn, but he'd had the feeling neither of them meant it. His father did — partly, because he had been able to unload the burden of guilt he had carried so long. But there was more to it than that.

Ross walked up the street. He didn't know where Milburn's office was. He stopped a young man he had never seen before and asked, "Know where Judge Milburn's office is?"

The young man looked startled, then stared at him with something of awe in his eyes. Ross grinned inwardly. The word that he was back had travelled fast. Even this man knew — guessed it was he because he had asked where Judge Milburn's office was.

The man said, "It's in the Vail Building next to the bank. Second floor, I think."

"Thanks." Ross went on up the street, passed the bank, and entered the Vail Building. He climbed the stairs. Visible from the head of them was a door with the gold-lettered legend on its glass, "Orville Milburn, Attorney-at-Law."

The lettering must have been there for a

long time, Ross thought. It must have been put there before Milburn became a judge. He opened the door.

There was a dark carpet on the floor and several heavy chairs of golden oak. A connecting door was open and he heard Orv Milburn's voice, "Be with you in a minute. Take a chair."

He sat down. A musty smell was in the air, the smell of books, and dry papers, and stale cigar smoke.

Milburn came to the connecting door. For an instant his face was blank. Then it took on a look of extreme affability. He crossed to Ross and gripped his hand. "Ross! Good to see you. Come on inside."

Ross followed him into the inner office. He sat down in the chair facing Milburn's desk. "You said you had some money that belonged to me."

"To you and your father. Yes. Have you seen him?"

"I've seen him. He's over at the barbershop getting cleaned up."

Milburn clucked. "Too bad. Too bad. Your conviction really hit him hard."

Ross didn't reply. He fixed his glance on Milburn's face unwaveringly, getting an obscure pleasure out of the way Milburn avoided it.

Milburn dug into his desk drawer and began fumbling with papers there. He came up with a sheaf of them and began thumbing through it. He cleared his throat. "Yes. Here it is. The balance coming to you is three hundred and twenty-four dollars and seventy-eight cents. I'll write you a cheque for it."

Ross didn't speak. Milburn seemed to be getting increasingly nervous. His hands shook as he wrote out the cheque, as he handed it to Ross. He met Ross's glance briefly, then looked away. The affability in his face was strained.

Ross said, "What's the matter, Judge? What are you so nervous about?"

"Paper work makes me nervous. Always did." He put out his hand to Ross. "That settles us up. Come up anytime though, Ross. Anything I can do to help . . ."

"Sure. I'll remember that." He tucked the cheque into his shirt pocket and went back out into the hall. He went down the stairs slowly. It would take more than this three hundred and some odd dollars to settle him up with Milburn. But even this would help right now. He needed clothes, a decent horse and a gun. His father needed things.

And the money meant he would no

longer have to work for Caine. He could spend his time hunting the trail he had come back to find.

He found his thoughts dwelling on Lily Caine. Her face — her eyes — they were as clear in his mind as though she were standing before him now.

He told himself any woman who was young and pretty would have affected him the same. Fifteen years in a world of men couldn't help but make him susceptible. But he knew it wasn't true. Any woman wouldn't have affected him the way Lily had. Some bond had been between them from the first instant their glances met.

He frowned thoughtfully as he went into the bank. Perhaps the bond existed only because both of them had been so badly used by their fellow men.

He went to the teller's window and fished the cheque from his pocket. The teller was young, someone he'd never seen before. Ross said, "I want to open an account. And I want a hundred of this in cash."

The teller handed him a pen and he endorsed the cheque. The teller looked at it, said nervously, "Just a minute, Mr. Logan," and disappeared.

Ross waited. A youth came from behind

the teller's cage and hurried out the front door. He came back several minutes later, out of breath. Shortly afterward, the uneasy teller reappeared and said with nervous heartiness, "Yes, Mr. Logan. Yes." He began to fill out an account card, entered the deposit, handed Ross a hundred dollars in ten-dollar bills and a receipt for the deposit.

Turning, Ross grinned sourly. The name Logan didn't inspire the trust and respect it once had in Horseshoe County. But it would. Before he was through it would be a respected name again.

Juan Mascarenas met him just outside the bank. He glanced at the money in Ross's hand. "The money Judge Milburn said he was holding for you?"

"Part of it. How much do you reckon it takes to keep an old man in grub and whisky in this town?"

"Twenty, thirty dollars a month I'd say. If he drank as much as Tom Logan does."

"Say twenty-five, then. For fifteen years that adds up to forty-five hundred dollars. Add the three hundred he just gave me and it's damn' near five thousand. A lot of strays and bad debts, wouldn't you say?"

"Speaks well for Judge Milburn's generosity, I'd say." Juan was watching him closely, a strange expression in his eyes.

Ross nodded thoughtfully. "You don't think it could be salve for a guilty conscience, do you?"

Mascarenas shrugged expressively. "You were Orv's first big case and he lost. Maybe he did feel bad about it and maybe he did have a guilty conscience, wondering if he'd done everything he could. It could explain a lot of salve."

"Maybe."

Mascarenas studied him and warned, "You're an ex-con, Ross. If you give the people hereabouts a chance, they'll probably accept you eventually. But if you're set on stirring up trouble, your record will be held against you in anything that happens."

Ross said bitterly, "My record! The only facts in my record are that I spent fifteen years in the pen for something I didn't do."

The sheriff shrugged. "I warned you, Ross."

"So you did." Ross crossed the street to the barbershop. Tom Logan was in the chair, his face lathered. Ross sat down. Two other men in the shop, strangers, studied him surreptitiously.

He waited patiently. He thought about Orv Milburn and he thought about Tobias Vail. He tried to remember everyone else who had been here fifteen years ago.

But his thoughts kept going back to Lily Caine and he kept remembering each small expression he had seen in her face during the short time he had known her. He told himself almost angrily, "She's a married woman. She's Caine's wife. She's not for you and you're a damn' fool for even thinking about her!"

The barber finished shaving his father. He raised the chair and began to cut his hair. Ross met his father's eyes and grinned. His father grinned back uncertainly.

His haircut finished, Tom Logan stepped down out of the chair. He crossed the room and stared at himself in the mirror. Ross could see the slight squaring of his shoulders.

He paid the barber and followed his father into the street.

A buckboard was whirling toward him half a block away. Ross stepped into the street and started across.

Tom Logan yelled, "Ross!"

He yanked his head around. The buckboard was only a dozen yards away, coming fast. Vail was driving and his whip snaked out . . .

Ross leaped back. A buckboard wheel struck him and knocked him rolling in the dust. The buckboard pulled up just beyond, the horses rearing, plunging . . .

Ross got up. He wasn't hurt but he was mad. Vail yelled, "Damn it, look where you're going! I told you to stay out of my way!"

Ross walked toward the buckboard slowly. When he reached it, he grabbed one of Vail's legs with both hands and dumped him neatly into the dust. He said, "You meant to do that, you son-of-a-bitch!"

Vail got up. His face was livid, his eyes burning. He swung recklessly at Ross.

Ross ducked the punch and swung one of his own, one that connected solidly. Vail was flung back against a buckboard wheel.

Ross stepped closer, waiting for Vail to recover. He felt his arms caught from behind. Mascarenas's voice said, "Easy now. Damn it, I told you to take it easy!"

Vail recovered. He lunged at Ross and his bony fist landed squarely on Ross's nose. It began to drop blood.

Ross struggled to free himself, but Mascarenas held on. The sheriff's strength was tremendous. Mascarenas yelled, "Mr. Vail!" but not before Vail's fist had landed in Ross's face a second time.

Vail stopped and stood motionless,

breathing hard, his face congested with blood. Mascarenas released Ross.

Ross said angrily, "He tried to run me down!" He stared at Vail. "You're packing a damn' big hate! Why? Could it be you had something to do with what happened fifteen years ago?"

A large vein in Vail's forehead swelled until Ross thought it would burst. Vail's face turned grey. Mascarenas said sharply, "Ross! Quit proddin' him! Can't you see . . . ?"

Vail staggered back, and supported himself against the buckboard wheel. Mascarenas shouted, "Get going, Ross! I mean it! I'll look after Mr. Vail!"

Ross whirled, went around the buckboard and crossed the street, his father hurrying to catch up. Behind him, he could hear Mascarenas talking to Vail. After a moment he heard Vail reply weakly something about not needing any damn' doctor. He walked up the street and entered Fetterman's General Store. As he did, the buckboard passed in the street behind him.

He turned his head. Vail was driving, his face rigid and straight ahead.

Ross said, "Come on, Pa."

He bought new clothes for himself and new clothes for his father. He bought a second-hand gun and belted holster to go with it, knowing even as he did that arming himself was dangerous.

But he knew it was equally dangerous to go unarmed. There was at least one man in Horseshoe County who wanted him dead. There were probably more than that.

He paid for his purchases and for those of his father and the two walked back toward Tom Logan's shack. Ross helped him to clean it out. It was sundown when they finished.

There was some grub in the cupboard, so Ross built up a fire and started supper. He felt stronger to-night than he had since his return. All he'd needed, he guessed, was a few square meals and the feel of freedom in his lungs.

Dusk came quickly to the town. Ross asked, "Want to ride out to Horseshoe with me? I ought to tell Caine I'm not going to work for him."

The old man shook his head. He stared at Ross apologetically. "I guess I don't want to look at Horseshoe yet."

Ross nodded and went outside. He untied his horse and mounted. He rode down the street in the direction of Horseshoe Ranch.

The same feeling he'd had riding in returned. It was as though hostility was tangible here in the street, in the soft dusk of the summer night.

Motion behind a building on his right caught his eye. An instant later he heard the unmistakable, metallic click of the cocking hammer of a gun.

He left his horse instantly, the muzzle flash over there bright in his eyes. He tasted dust, and felt his impact with the ground.

The gun muzzle flashed again, closer, and again.

Ross waited, gun in hand, and motionless in the dust. He saw the shadowy figure raise the gun for a final, killing shot.

He fired instantly. He heard the solid impact of the bullet hard on the heels of the report.

The other man's gun clattered to the street. He doubled, holding his stomach with both hands as though he had a stomach ache. He folded quietly forward and lay still in the dusty street less than a dozen feet away.

Ross got up, holstering his gun. His horse stood nervously about fifty feet from him. He could hear footsteps running toward him and, looking up, saw the bulky form of Juan Mascarenas leading them.

He holstered his gun but he kept his hand on it. If anybody thought they were going to railroad him again, they were wrong. Juan said, "Ross! Goddam it, I knew it meant trouble when you rode into town."

Ross said sourly, "Go turn him over and see who the hell he is. Then maybe you can tell me why he tried to murder me."

Chapter Six

Someone, at Mascarenas's direction, ran and got a lantern. He came back, the lantern flickering, casting a yellow light around the man carrying it.

In this yellow light, Juan Mascarenas seemed obese, like a carved Chinese figure Ross had seen once in a shop window in the prison town. The sheriff's face was shining with an oily sweat generated by his run here from the jail.

He went to the dead man and turned him over callously with a foot. He grunted, "Never seen him before."

Ross felt the taste of defeat. This man might be a stranger but there had to be a thread connecting him to someone hereabouts. He said, "Have the others look at him. Maybe someone's seen him before."

The sheriff called, "You folks mind coming over here and taking a look at this man? He tried to kill Mr. Logan and I'd like to find out who he is."

They approached reluctantly. Mascarenas held the lantern close to the dead man's face, but he watched the faces of those who stopped and stared down at it.

Ross watched them too. He felt shaken, for this was the first man he had ever killed. He'd come close, once while he was in prison, in a fight with another prisoner but . . .

A man dressed in range clothes stepped up. Ross saw the recognition in his features instantly. Juan asked, "Know him?"

"Wouldn't say I knew him. I saw him once a couple of days ago."

"Where was this?"

"Out at the ranch. He drifted in and asked me for a job. I turned him down."

Ross asked, "Whose ranch?"

The man turned to look at him, but he did not reply. Mascarenas said, "Vail's." He turned his head and stared at the man. "Where'd he go?"

"Rode out again, heading for town. He asked where it was and how big it was and then headed for it. I never saw him again until now."

Ross interrupted, "Was Vail there at the time?"

"Yeah. He was in the house."

The sheriff said, "All right, Luke. Thanks.

By the way, this is Ross Logan. Luke Pierson, Ross. He's Vail's foreman."

Pierson stuck out a hand and Ross gripped it. He asked, "Vail didn't leave soon after this man was there, did he?"

Mascarenas said sharply, "Ross! Just because you'd like to pin something on Vail . . ."

Ross said, "Did he?"

"Not right away. It was a couple of hours at least before he left."

Ross nodded. He looked at the sheriff. "Any charges against me for this?"

Mascarenas shook his head. "I doubt it." He picked up the stranger's gun and spun the cylinder. "Three empties. Lemme see yours."

Ross handed it to him. The sheriff examined his gun. "Shot once, huh?"

Ross nodded. Mascarenas grunted, "No charges. Pure and simple self-defence. All right?"

Ross nodded again. He said, "If I'd been guilty, there'd be no reason for anyone trying to kill me, would there?"

Mascarenas said impatiently, "Oh, for Christ's sake, Ross! This doesn't prove anything. This man might have mistaken you for someone else. And even if what you're trying to say is so, even if someone here did hire him to kill you, what does it prove? Maybe someone doesn't think fifteen years is enough. Maybe they think you should have been executed."

"What do you think, Sheriff?"

Mascarenas stared directly into his face. "I think if you didn't do it, like you say, that fifteen years was too much."

"And if I did?"

Mascarenas turned away without answering. He said, "Two or three of you take the body over to Mace Rossiter's. Tell Mace we'll have an inquest there at ten in the morning."

Ross walked to his horse. Mace Rossiter had been both the County Coroner and the undertaker for as long as he could recall. He had buried Ruth.

He swung astride. Without speaking to the sheriff again, he rode on out of town.

Maybe this attempt on his life didn't prove anything to Juan, but it proved something to him. It proved that the killer was still here. It proved that Ross's presence had made him nervous, just as Ross had figured it would.

A thought suddenly struck him that made him feel weak inside. What if he hadn't bought a gun this afternoon? What if he'd been unarmed?

Frowning soberly, he rode toward Horseshoe, and discovered that he had begun thinking of Lily Caine again.

Strange, the way her face was so clear in his mind. Strange, too, the way she was so much in his thoughts. He shook his head impatiently. He had better get her out of his mind. There was nothing but grief for both of them if he let himself become involved with her.

He rode in at the Horseshoe about nine o'clock. A single light was burning in the kitchen. He rode to the door and dismounted. Caine had gone over earlier to see Sadie Plue about a new bunch of broncs, but he ought to be back by now. He knocked.

Lily opened the door. Seeing him, fright touched her eyes briefly and then was gone. Ross said, "Your husband here?"

She shook her head. Her voice was low, throaty, subdued. "No. Someone came out from town and told him Judge Milburn wanted to see him. That was about six. He isn't back yet."

"I . . . I wanted to tell him I wasn't going to work for him."

Her expression changed almost imperceptibly. "Won't you come in?"

"I'd better not. If he'd come back . . . I

mean, after the things he said . . ." Embarrassment touched him and he felt confused.

She murmured, "Then I'll come out."

She did, leaving the door open. She stood on the sagging stoop staring at the sky. Her face was in shadow, but the light behind her made a kind of halo of her hair.

The compulsion to touch her, to hold her in his arms, was almost overpowering. Ross asked, "What's Caine's connection with the judge?"

She turned her head. She had not been thinking of Caine. He wished he knew what she had been thinking. She said, "Judge Milburn owns this ranch. We just live here and look after it. My husband breaks horses for the army."

"Are you sure?" Her statement that Caine didn't own Horseshoe came as a shock to him. If Milburn owned it . . .

That opened up a whole new field of conjecture. And the fact that Caine had been in town to-night . . . Caine might have been behind the attempt on his life; he might have hired the stranger and pointed Ross out to him.

He said, "I didn't know that," feeling sure it was something neither Milburn nor Caine wanted him to know.

"I don't know whether I should have told you. You won't tell my husband?"

He said, "I won't tell him." He could see the fear in her upturned face. Her eyes were wide with it. He found himself hating Caine more than he had before.

He took a step toward her and she backed away from him. He said, "I'm sorry. I guess . . . you know about me, don't you?"

"I know you're Ross Logan. I know that you used to live here and that you spent fifteen years in jail for killing your wife."

"Is that why you're afraid of me?"

"I . . ." Her voice was scarcely audible and she wouldn't look at him. Then she raised her glance determinedly. She said staunchly, "I don't think you killed her." She seemed confused and afraid. "I had better go inside."

Ross nodded. She backed into the doorway. Light touched her features. Their glances locked and held, and for an instant Ross held his breath. Then he said harshly, "I won't be seeing you again," knowing even as he said it that it wasn't true. He would see her again. Something was between them that couldn't be denied.

She replied, "No. Good-bye." She didn't close the door so Ross turned away and picked up his horse's reins. He stared at her, at her finely made face, at her eyes, her mouth. He said, "Tell him that I won't be back."

"All right." There was a certain lifelessness now about her voice. She closed the door.

Ross mounted, but for a moment he sat on his horse, holding him still. Her face as he had seen it last was etched on his brain and he knew it would remain. He whirled his horse suddenly and galloped out of the yard.

He wanted to turn, ride back and burst into the house. He wanted to seize her in his arms and hold her and . . .

His skin felt hot. That was how it must have been with Ruth. As beautiful as she had been . . . as capable of stirring a man up. She had made them want her the way he wanted Lily Caine.

Suddenly he felt unclean. His feelings toward Lily were as sordid as those of Ruth's lovers had been toward her. Lily was Caine's wife. Nothing was going to change that fact. If he touched her he'd be no better than the man he was hunting now. Except that he'd never kill.

But there was a difference. He seized it and clung to it in his thoughts. Lily Caine wasn't Ruth. She wasn't like Ruth at all. She'd not encouraged him and she never would. She might be miserable with Caine — she had to be — but it was a bargain she herself had made and she obviously had no intention of breaking it.

To be treated like a woman — to have consideration shown for her feelings and her thoughts — these were new experiences to her and naturally had their effect on her.

He told himself it was nothing more than that but he knew it wasn't true. For an instant back there, while their glances locked, the same bond had been between them and it was a bond that nothing would ever break.

He forced himself to think of Milburn and Caine, wondering why he had not suspected that Milburn owned Horseshoe Ranch. Hell, the man hadn't sold it to pay for the expenses of the trial. Or if he had, he'd simply sold it to a dummy who had immediately re-sold it to him.

He himself had set the price. It hadn't been a *bona fide* offer at all. Then he'd taken the money he'd paid for it to satisfy his fee and the court costs.

Ross's father, perhaps already drinking to forget his guilt, tormented by his son's predicament and his own inability to help, had neither known nor cared what happened to the cattle and the ranch.

But Milburn had a conscience too. He had given Ross three hundred and some-odd dollars of conscience money to-day.

He frowned. Juan Mascarenas had been right. The attempt on his life didn't prove Ruth's killer was still around. It only proved that someone hated him or feared him enough to want him dead.

Milburn might be the one. Or Tobias Vail might be. Or Caine because he had already sensed the bond between Ross Logan and his wife.

One thing he did know — whoever had tried to kill him would try again.

Lily Caine's statement that Milburn owned Horseshoe had opened up a whole new field of thought for Ross. Perhaps Horseshoe could be recovered if it could be proved that Milburn had acted fraudulently in obtaining it. He touched his horse's ribs with his heels and the animal broke into a sluggish trot.

Chapter Seven

Tom Logan was not at the shack when Ross arrived. He cursed softly under his breath.

Then he shrugged philosophically. He could hardly expect his father to give up liquor, which had been his crutch for fifteen years, in a single day. It wouldn't be that easy and he had no right to expect it to be.

He was tired, but he did not go to bed. Instead, he closed the door and walked up the street toward the Antlers Saloon, suddenly struck by a parallel between his father and Ruth. Perhaps she hadn't been able to help herself any more than his father could.

Tom Logan was at the bar. He was talking to Orv Milburn, who stood at his right.

Ross came up on the other side. Tom Logan's eyes were bloodshot and he was very drunk. Ross said, "Let's go home, Pa."

His father turned his head and peered at

him. He said, "We're celebratin'."

"Celebrating what?"

"You comin' home."

Ross stared angrily at Milburn. "This your idea?"

"Now, Ross, I like your Pa. We get together like this every once in a while."

"Sure. You've been doing it for fifteen years, haven't you? Keep him loaded with whisky and he doesn't have time to think."

Tom Logan stared uncomprehendingly from one to the other. Ross said, "I've been doing a little arithmetic. I've been adding it up — what it takes to keep a man alive and loaded with whisky for fifteen years. It comes to about five thousand dollars. That's a lot of strays and bad debts, Judge. Don't you think it is?"

Milburn's eyes were angrily defiant. "That's what a man gets . . . just because I couldn't stand by and see him starve . . ."

Ross asked, "You got anything to hide, Judge?"

Milburn's face turned pink. His eyes were angry, but they did not meet Ross's squarely. He blustered, "I don't have to stand here and listen to this kind of talk. I'm sorry I lost your case. But you killed her, Ross, and there's a limit to what a defence attorney can do."

"Oh. You think I killed her. You're sure of it. Did you feel that way while you were defending me?"

"A man can't help what he believes."

"But a defence attorney who doesn't believe his client's innocence . . . he wouldn't have much chance of proving it, would he?"

"I did my best . . ."

"Maybe you did, Judge. That's what I want to find out. In the meantime, stay away from Pa."

He took his father's arm, turned him and headed for the door. The batwings swung and a man entered.

He was a big man, taller than Ross, his hair, straw yellow, was beginning to thin above his forehead. He was heavier than he had been last time Ross saw him and there were new lines in his face.

The man grinned delightedly and came rushing across the intervening space. He shouted, "Ross! Dammit, I'm glad to see you! Heard this afternoon that you were back. I've been . . . Well, hell, you don't care about that."

He slapped Ross on the shoulder with his left hand as he took Ross's outstretched hand with his right.

Ross returned his grin. Phil's face was

open, friendly, very familiar even after all this time.

Ross had gone to school with Phil. He'd fished and hunted and worked with him. He couldn't remember when he hadn't known Phil.

And Phil was the only one, except for his father, who'd stuck by him during the trial. He was one of the very few who had bothered to write, even occasionally, while Ross was in prison.

Still pumping his hand, Phil said, "Remember the time you straddled that buck to cut his throat and he got up and began to run with you?" He began to laugh, remembering how ridiculous Ross had looked, but there was an underlying seriousness in his eyes as well.

Ross remembered, all right. All kinds of memories came flooding back. But the strongest thing in him right now was gratitude at being greeted warmly for a change. Instead of warily, or reluctantly, or angrily.

His throat tight, he said, "Come on down to Pa's place. We've got a lot of catching up to do."

"Sure. I'll be right along. I'll pick up a bottle first."

Ross nodded, warmed by the encounter.

Then he went out, still holding his father's arm.

The streets were nearly deserted. The air was cool and there was a breeze blowing from the southwest. It carried a smell of the loading corrals at the foot of Main.

The broadwalk sounded hollowly beneath their feet. Tom Logan made an effort to walk steadily but he was not successful.

Frowning, Ross tried to sort in his mind those he suspected of hiring the stranger to shoot him down. He asked, "Did you hear the shooting down at the lower end of town right after I left to ride out to Horseshoe?"

"Uh-huh. Time I got there, though, you were gone."

"Got any ideas who might have hired him to take a shot at me?"

"Vail, mebbe . . . after what happened earlier."

Ross guided him through the weeds to the shack door. He opened it. He lighted a lamp, hearing hard-pounding hoofbeats in the street as he did. They stopped before he could reach the door.

His father staggered across the room and collapsed on the bed. Ross covered him and pulled off his boots. He stood for a moment, staring down.

Ruth had certainly left a wreckage of human lives behind her when she died, he thought. He wondered if his father would ever be the same again, or if he would himself.

Phil would be along soon. He built up the fire and put some coffee on. He could hear shouting somewhere up the street.

He sat down and stared at the open door. The breeze entered through it, blew across him and out the open window at his back.

Freedom had a loose, easy feel to it that he never got tired of savouring. There were no bars at that open door, or at the window behind him. Bars would never shut him in again.

He heard the weeds rustling in front of the shack and yelled, "Come on in. The coffee's on."

Juan Mascarenas appeared at the door. For an instant Ross's face was startled. There was a gun in Mascarenas's hand.

Ross asked, "What the hell is that for? Change your mind about that shooting a while ago?"

The sheriff stepped through the door warily. His face had an oily shine to it. His dark eyes were narrowed, hard as tiny bits of stone. He said, "Easy now, Ross. Just unbuckle that gunbelt and let it slide to the floor. Kick it aside."

Ross didn't move. He stared at Mascarenas's face. There was something in it . . . something not at all professional, something almost personal . . .

He could feel anger stirring in the back of his mind. Horseshoe County hadn't exactly put out the welcome mat for him. Caine had beaten him first. Someone had tried to kill him a while ago and Vail had tried to run him down. Now this. And he'd only just come home.

He said, "Suppose you tell me what this is all about."

"Shuck your gun, Ross. I don't want to shoot you down."

"Not until . . ."

Mascarenas's voice was like a whip. "Ross!"

Ross looked him steadily in the eye. He said evenly, "All right, shoot, God damn you! But don't expect me to give myself up when you haven't even bothered to tell me what I'm supposed to have done!"

Hesitation touched the sheriff's face. In the utter silence, Ross heard Phil Rivers whistling as he came along down the street.

The sheriff heard it too but he didn't turn his head. He started to edge away from the door, keeping his eyes steadily on Ross.

On the couch, Ross's father suddenly released an explosive snore. Mascarenas started, and his glance switched to Tom Logan on the couch.

Ross drew his gun smoothly, cocking the hammer as he did. The sheriff's glance switched back to him. Ross grinned mockingly. "Mexican stand-off now, Juan. What are you going to do about it? Phil will be here in another half a minute."

"This ain't going to get you nothing, Ross. You killed Caine and you'll go to the gallows for it."

Ross stared. "Why? For Christ's sake, why would I kill Caine?"

"Because he beat the hell out of you out there at Horseshoe where you figured you belonged. And because you wanted his wife. He told Orv Milburn that you'd taken a shine to her."

Ross said furiously, "I wouldn't be *that* big a fool!" He stared at the sheriff's unrelenting face. He heard Rivers's footsteps in the weeds outside the shack.

He said, "You're going to have to shoot that gun or drop it. I'm not stupid enough to let you put me in jail. I wouldn't have a chance this time. So if I'm going to die I'll do it my way, right here and now."

Mascarenas's gun dropped to the floor as Phil appeared in the doorway behind him. Phil looked startled. "What's going on?"

"Juan claims I killed Caine." There was a hollow, aching feeling inside Ross's chest. He'd come home to find out who had really killed Ruth, to vindicate himself. And this was how it was going to end. He didn't dare surrender himself; he wouldn't have a chance. So he'd run — and every hand in the county would be against him. Mascarenas had dropped his gun a moment before because he knew when he'd been outmanœuvred. But Juan was as cagey on a trail as any Indian ever was, and Juan would come after him. Ross would run until he dropped.

But he wasn't going to prison again and he wasn't going to hang. He'd already paid with fifteen years of his life for something he hadn't done. This time they'd have to kill him because he wasn't going to be taken alive.

He picked up the sheriff's gun. He walked to the door and turned. He said thinly, "Don't follow me, Juan. If you do, I'll kill you."

Rivers's voice was sober. "Don't worry

about him, Ross. I'll keep him here until you get out of town."

Mascarenas sighed. "This won't make any difference, Phil. We'll get him anyway. But if I take him now, at least he'll be alive."

Ross interrupted bitterly, "For how long, Juan? Until you can get a scaffold built?" He backed out the door, stepped aside and was swallowed by darkness instantly.

He ran through the thick, high weeds. There was the sound of voices up the street, and then the sound of many boots approaching along the hollow-sounding walk. Phil wasn't going to be able to hold Mascarenas until he got out of town.

As silently as he could, Ross ran to the alley and along it to First Street at its end. He followed the street to Main, then turned toward the livery barn.

A solitary horse tied to a rail in front of a darkened shack caught his eye. He went to it and unwound the reins. He mounted and pounded away.

A door slammed open and an outraged voice yelled, "Hey! come back here with my horse!"

Ross didn't turn his head. Urging the horse to a hard gallop, he cleared the limits of the town. He headed south aimlessly.

Where he could go, where he could find food and refuge, he hadn't the faintest idea. How he could now vindicate himself of guilt in two murders, he had even less idea. He could only travel, and hide, and travel some more. If he was caught, it meant either prison bars again or the hangman's noose.

Chapter Eight

Ross had spent fifteen years in prison but he had never been hunted before and the feeling was new to him.

He would need supplies, food, extra clothing, ammunition. He would need a fresh horse.

He frowned in the darkness, trying to think of places where he might obtain these things.

It was difficult to think clearly. Too much had happened too suddenly. He hadn't even known Caine was dead and now he was running because he had been accused of killing him.

He had no illusions. He was virtually friendless in a county that had once been home to him. Sadie Plue, dried up and horsy and usually at odds with the law, was the only one he could think of who might conceivably give him food and a fresh horse. Where else he might go . . .

He knew suddenly where he could go.

Horseshoe. Lily Caine would believe him when he said he'd had nothing to do with her husband's death.

But going there was dangerous. It was one of the first places Juan would look for him. It was even possible, though not too likely, that Juan had already sent someone to Horseshoe to wait for him.

Faintly, behind him, he could hear the town's outcry. The bell on top of the courthouse began to toll as Juan Mascarenas began to round up a posse. Shouts, and an occasional exuberant shot, came to him dimly on the slight northerly breeze.

He kicked the horse into a steady run. There wasn't much chance that they'd try picking up his trail and following him in the dark. Not when dawn was only three hours away.

But Juan would be coming after him at dawn. With a posse — probably a big one at the start. Only if the posse failed to catch Ross in a couple of days by splitting up and thoroughly scouring the countryside would Juan release them and come on by himself. Juan himself would never quit. Ross remembered once, years ago, when Juan had stayed on a killer's trail for more than a month. And he'd brought the killer back with him.

His mind kept going over those who might have been guilty of killing Caine, over those who might have been guilty of killing Ruth. Then his mouth twisted wryly. There wasn't much point now in trying to solve either crime. Nobody was going to believe anything he said. He was an ex-con, guilty in the mind of everyone of Ruth's killing, now guilty of a second one. They had expected him to show humility upon his return and he hadn't. He'd been quarrelsome and truculent instead.

The horse he was riding wasn't exactly fresh. He'd probably been ridden into town from some outlying ranch only this afternoon. But Ross pushed him hard, to the limit of the animal's endurance. He ran him, then walked him briefly, then ran him again. How much speed he made, how much ground he covered these first few hours, might make the difference between being caught and getting away later in the day.

An hour before dawn, he saw the dark buildings of Horseshoe ahead of him.

He slowed the horse instantly to a walk. He rode in silently, and left the horse while he was still a hundred yards from the nearest building.

Walking carefully, he approached. Watchfully he circled the barn and went inside. If they were waiting for him here, their horses would have been hidden in the barn.

But there was nothing. The place, smelling faintly of dry manure, leather and hay dust, was silent as a tomb.

He went back into the chilling air of approaching dawn. He stared briefly at the house, for the moment assailed by doubt. Why should Lily Caine believe anything he said? Why should she give him help? Perhaps he had deluded himself into believing that the attraction between them was mutual, that she also felt the instantaneous bond he did whenever their glances locked.

But he knew he had little choice. It was Lily Caine or Sadie Plue. And he needed a fresh horse *now*.

He returned to his horse, mounted and rode directly to the house. He dismounted and knocked on the kitchen door.

A minute passed. Then he saw the faintest flicker of light inside, light that grew stronger as Lily Caine approached, carrying a lamp. The door opened.

She stood framed in it, startled, wearing nightgown and wrapper. Her hair was in braids. She had been in bed but it was obvious that she had not been asleep.

Her eyes clung to his face for an instant and then she said worriedly, "Ross! Come in. Has anything happened? Is something wrong?"

It was the first time she had used his given name and it had a sound no one had ever given it before. He went inside and Lily closed the door. She crossed the room and put the lamp down on the table. Then she turned to face him.

She searched his face for a moment before she said, "Something *is* wrong. What is it, Ross?"

"Your husband's dead," he said harshly. "And I've been accused of killing him." He put it bluntly, almost cruelly, and watched her face closely afterwards for signs of doubt.

There were none. But there was dismay, and instant fear. She cried, "You? Accused of . . . ? But that's ridiculous! What possible reason . . . ?" She stopped, a slow flush creeping into her face.

Ross nodded wryly. "They say I killed him because of the beating he gave me. And because I wanted you."

For an instant she was completely defenceless. Her voice was almost a whisper. "Do you, Ross?"

"You know I do."

Her eyes were stricken as she stared at him. "I'm sorry, Ross. I'm so awfully sorry. Because of me, you're in trouble again."

"It would have come anyway. Someone doesn't want me around. If it hadn't been Caine who was killed, it would have been someone else. And I'd have been accused of it."

"Do you have any idea . . . ?"

He nodded. "Judge Milburn is the most logical one. Caine knew how he got title to this ranch. The judge might have killed him to keep him quiet about it."

She began to build up the fire almost automatically. She pulled the coffee pot to the front of the stove where it would heat. Ross thought sourly that Milburn wasn't the only one who wanted to be rid of him. Vail was another and he didn't make any bones about it. Juan Mascarenas hadn't exactly been overjoyed to see him return.

Worry was strong in Lily's face and eyes. "Where will you go? Where *can* you go? If they catch you now . . ."

He shook his head. "I don't know yet what I'm going to do. Right now I've got to keep ahead of them. Can you fix me up with a sack of supplies?"

"Of course." She got a flour sack from a drawer, then moved swiftly around the kitchen, filling it with things he would need.

He watched her for a moment hungrily, realising suddenly how much he had missed over the past fifteen years. The softness that a woman contributes to the life of a man. The unquestioning faith she can give to him. Once Lily turned her head and smiled at him as though sensing his thoughts, then looked away and went back to her work. There was a slight, persistent flush on her face and he understood its cause.

He said almost harshly, "I'll need a fresh horse."

"Do you need to ask? Don't you know . . ." She did not finish.

Ross said, "All right." He went out into the darkness.

There was a dampness to the air now that told him dawn was not very far away. He walked to the corral, took down a rope and stood for a moment, listening. Then he stepped in through the gate and roped out the chunky grey he had broken his first day here.

He led the animal to where he'd left his own mount and quickly changed saddle and bridle to the grey. He turned the other horse loose, knowing he would eventually return to wherever he belonged. He mounted the grey, certain the animal would buck and wanting this over with before he left.

The horse didn't disappoint him. He bucked determinedly for several minutes before he stopped.

Ross slid off and tied the reins. He re-entered the house.

Lily had the sack ready for him. She also had Caine's rifle and a good supply of shells for it. She stood with her back to the stove, watching him.

He crossed the room to the chair where she had laid the sack and against which the rifle leaned, but he did not immediately pick them up. He stared across the room at her, watching the pulse that beat in her throat, trying to read the expression in her face and eyes.

He had not imagined that strong, unspoken bond between them. It was there; it would always be there. He knew he ought to leave, that time was slipping rapidly away, important time, but he stood there frozen for a moment more.

Lily whispered, "I am ashamed . . . I know I should be grieving for him but I can't. Ross, I just can't. He married me as he would buy a horse — because he needed one. I didn't know that at first, but

I knew it . . . later. I'm sorry that his death was violent and that he died alone. But . . ."

Ross didn't reply. There seemed to be nothing he could say.

Her voice was now scarcely audible. "Will I ever see you again?"

He nodded firmly. "I'm not leaving the county yet. And even if I should, you'll hear from me. You know that, don't you?"

She nodded wordlessly.

He said, "I didn't kill Caine. But I might have, eventually."

She did not speak. Ross knew this moment was important to them both. He knew it was important that she understand that he wanted her, that he would come back to her.

But suddenly, meeting her unwavering glance, he knew she understood. And he understood something about her as well. In her thoughts she had already given herself to him. She would wait. She would be here when he came back. Already she had given him the unquestioning faith he so badly needed.

And she was worried about him, desperately worried. That showed in her eyes too, and in the trembling of her lower lip. She would go with him now if he asked her to. She would share with him whatever the future held, either good or bad.

There was a tightness in his throat as he said, "Good-bye, Lily."

"Good-bye, Ross."

He picked up the sack and the rifle. With his free hand, he stuffed the ammunition into his pocket. He glanced at her briefly, then turned toward the door.

It was almost physically painful for him to leave without touching her. Not when he wanted to so desperately.

He stepped outside. There was a grey streak in the east, but it was still too dark to trail. In another fifteen minutes they'd be leaving town, following his trail. He couldn't linger here another moment.

He mounted, and glanced down at Lily standing just outside the door. There were tears in her eyes now, and terror for his safety. She whispered, "God be with you, Ross, and keep you safe."

He didn't trust himself to reply. He swung the grey and rode away.

From a distance of a couple of hundred yards, he looked around. He supposed she could see him yet, silhouetted against the lightening sky. She stood just as he had left her, straight, still, and he had a strange feeling that her lips were moving soundlessly.

He turned his head and went on. When he looked back again the house was out of sight below a rise of ground.

She had warmed him with her concern, strengthened him with her faith. She had given him the physical things he needed, food and a fresh horse, but she had given him much more important things.

He'd come back here to fight for his former, rightful place in the community. He had come back, as well, for revenge.

Those things suddenly paled into insignificance before this new thing he had found.

There was something worthwhile to fight for now. He knew that no matter how they hounded him, he would never leave. Not even if staying was to cost him his life.

Chapter Nine

The whole sky had now turned grey. Heavy dew lay upon the grass. Ross's clothes felt damp.

He ran the grey steadily for several miles, working off the high spirits and rebellion not completely dispelled by the bucking session in the yard at Horseshoe. As the sun poked its golden rim above the horizon in the east, he slowed the lathered horse to a walk.

It might be a long time before he got another horse. This one's endurance and stamina would decide whether he was caught or not.

Occasionally he looked behind. He saw nothing. In mid-morning he climbed the rocky side of Cheyenne Ridge and, at its crest, turned his horse and squinted out across the sun-washed plain.

He could see for nearly twenty miles. And he could see, like a puff, a wisp, a wraith, the pillar of dust that rose from the hoofs of the horses carrying the posse.

They were all of fifteen miles away. He turned the grey and rode west now along the ridge's crest, for the first time riding where his trail would be hard to find.

Outwitting Juan Mascarenas was going to be difficult, if not impossible. His last fifteen years had been spent in prison while Juan's had been spent in the open, following the trails of fugitives. Juan's skill had been considerable fifteen years ago. It would be even greater now.

Suddenly Ross began to smile grimly. There was a way to make Juan get rid of his posse, at least.

He continued westward until he reached the edge of the badlands, then turned north again. In late afternoon he reached a point directly west of town and here turned east toward it.

The sun sank steadily into the badlands he had so recently left. In its last light, reflected from a few high, thin clouds, he found the wide, hard-beaten trail Mascarenas's posse had made leaving town at dawn to-day. He turned into it, urging his horse to the same speed the posse had been travelling so that his tracks would not be so clearly distinguishable from the others.

Juan might follow his trail in this jumble of other prints. But none of the others could and he figured Juan would send them home.

This way, he travelled for half a dozen miles. He passed Horseshoe with a hungry glance at the faint, flickering lights coming from the windows of the house. He went on until he was halfway to Cheyenne Ridge.

Here, he turned into a dry wash, the floor of which was rocky. Letting his horse pick a dainty, high-stepping way between the rocks, he rode along the wash for several miles before he stopped.

He picketed the grey on the plain, west of the wash, then rolled himself in his blankets on its edge.

There was a faint fragrance to the blankets that reminded him of Lily Caine. He closed his eyes exhaustedly, too tired even to eat. And he was instantly asleep.

Night noises awoke him several times, each time to lie still while his hand eased toward the grips of his gun. Each time he went back to sleep when he realised what had awakened him.

An hour before dawn he was up again, travelling eastward along the wash which lay far enough below the level of the plain to conceal both himself and his horse.

He hoped his trick of doubling back and riding in the posse's trail would make Juan send the posse back to town. He could cope with Juan. One man was predictable, and with but one man following there was less chance of blundering into the pursuit by accident.

He followed the wash steadily until noon, knowing where it led, and shortly after the sun passed its zenith, came out of the wash, grown shallower now, and climbed the side of Cheyenne Ridge half a dozen miles east of the place where he had climbed it yesterday.

He dismounted here and tied his horse. He got grub from the sack tied behind the saddle and, squatting comfortably in the shade of a towering rock, ate for the first time since leaving town.

He was ravenous, but he did not eat his fill. As he ate, his eyes kept sweeping the plain lazily but intently.

He saw no dust. But he saw a single, tiny speck crawling along the rim of the wash six or seven miles away.

He smiled briefly. Juan. He had disbanded the posse as Ross had hoped he would. He was coming on by himself, dogged, patient, unhurried. He wouldn't press Ross hard, but he'd come on steadily and he would never quit.

If Ross could keep Juan slavishly following trail, he could stay ahead of him. But if the sheriff ever guessed his destination at any time he'd ride ahead and be waiting when Ross arrived.

He angled aimlessly along the crest of Cheyenne Ridge, hiding his trail skilfully. He rode unhurriedly, at a pace just slightly faster than Juan's would be.

A game. A deadly game, with each man trying to outguess the other while Ross hid his trail and Mascarenas unravelled it. The thought of ambushing the sheriff occurred to Ross, but he discarded it immediately. He wasn't a killer, in spite of what Juan and the rest of the county's inhabitants thought of him. He wouldn't kill Juan even if his freedom depended upon it.

In mid-afternoon he left the ridge where a long, shallow draw cut away from it. He left prints plainly in the soft dust here, and rode for about a mile before he turned and climbed the slope. He crossed over, backtracked and returned to the top of Cheyenne Ridge.

Smiling faintly, he found a place from which he could see the draw and waited.

Juan Mascarenas came into sight, riding

slowly, head down as he studied the ground. Where Ross's trail turned off the ridge he stopped, and carefully surveyed the countryside ahead for nearly ten minutes. Ross's smile widened as he reined his horse aside and continued west. Juan had fallen for his ruse.

The sheriff was wary of an ambush as Ross wanted him to be. He would waste at least thirty minutes, watchfully scanning the land before he rode into it. And Ross would gain that thirty minutes, besides irritating Mascarenas immeasurably.

Scouting back and forth, he found the trail he had made riding the crest of this ridge yesterday. In many places it was obscured by the prints of the posse that had been pursuing him, but in others it was decipherable, because the posse had been spread out.

There were places, many of them, where two or three of the posse members had cut away from the trail for a better view of the plain. When he came to these, Ross put his horse into each of the trails leaving the main trail, returning when they returned.

The ruses wouldn't fool Juan, but they would cost him time. Time enough, perhaps, so that Ross could sleep safely again to-night.

But Juan could play the game as long as he. Juan knew that, sooner or later, Ross would have to have a fresh horse and a fresh supply of food.

When that time came . . . Juan knew the places Ross could go. Sadie Plue's. Or Horseshoe. Or town in the dead of night to break into a store or steal a horse from the livery barn.

At sundown, Ross was deep in the badlands west of Sadie Plue's. As dusk began to fade into the velvet darkness of night, he watered his horse at a thin, alkali stream, then urged him up the slope of the highest knoll he could see.

There was a little dry grass on the north side of the knoll, and Ross picketed the horse here. Then he climbed afoot to the top of the knoll, ate from his dwindling supply of food, and stretched himself out on the ground.

He was tired and discouragement was strong in him. Why was he running? What did he hope to gain by it? He couldn't spend his life running away from Juan Mascarenas and he didn't dare to stop.

Something must be done to free him from the necessity. If he intended to stay in the county, then he had better find out who really killed Caine.

That was first. That would take the pressure off. Afterward, if he could, he would try finding out who had killed Ruth fifteen years before.

But he couldn't do either while Mascarenas was on his trail. Somehow he had to lose him, for a day and a night at least.

He frowned in the darkness. An ambush seemed the only way. Perhaps an ambush was the way. He didn't have to kill Juan, or even wound him. All he had to do was kill his horse. Put him afoot far enough from Vail so that it would take him a couple of days to walk back.

After that he slept, awaking just before dawn, a habit deeply ingrained in him over the years spent in the prison. He ate sparingly of what food was left, mounted and headed deeper into the badlands to the west.

This was wild horse country, where Sadie Plue's sons trapped the wild ones they had sold to Caine. It stretched away for fifty miles and Ross rode straight west all day, taking no pains to hide his trail. He would make it look to Juan as though he had decided to leave the county after all. Believing that, Juan would hurry, and perhaps grow careless as he did.

An hour before sundown, Ross stopped.

He swung right, rode half a mile, and then began to backtrack carefully. The sun was a brassy ball on the western horizon when he finally found the place he sought.

He tied his horse and climbed a bare, shaley knoll afoot. Below him he could plainly see the trail he had made scarcely more than an hour before.

He lay down and made himself as comfortable as he could. His body was tired and stiff from riding, but the effects of Caine's beating and of the bronc busting he'd done were practically gone. He was hungry, but he wasn't weak. Strength was growing in him as his body adjusted itself to this new kind of life.

The sun went down, staining the clouds a brilliant gold that faded to shades of orange and pink and lavender. Dusk was slow in coming and Ross wasn't sure that Juan would be along to-night.

But just as the last light was fading from the sky, he heard the squeak of saddle leather and shortly afterward saw Juan come into sight.

The sheriff was riding at a trot for here the trail was easy to follow, even in grey dusk.

When the sheriff was directly below him, he deliberately levered a shell into the chamber of the rifle Lily Caine had given him.

The sound seemed as loud as a thunderclap in this silent place. Juan Mascarenas's head jerked around and he didn't hesitate. He left his horse with a swift, smooth movement, and was rolling toward the shelter of a clump of scrub brush even as he struck the ground.

He had done precisely what Ross wanted him to, exactly what Ross had expected him to do. Ross raised the rifle and sighted carefully.

The shot roared shockingly, its echoes picked up and bounced back by the surrounding hills. The bullet, striking the sheriff's horse, made a solid, meaty sound.

The horse went down, his forelegs folding first. Ross was moving back before he stopped kicking on the ground.

He had no way of knowing how soon Juan would figure out that Ross had only intended to kill his horse. But he had tremendous respect for Juan's ability. He knew his time was short.

Running crouched, he reached his horse and vaulted to the saddle. He sank his spurs.

The startled animal sprang ahead, and as he did a shot bellowed at Ross from behind. Then he rounded a knoll, thundered down a draw, and crashed through a thicket of brush.

From behind him came a bitter, monotonous cursing.

Mascarenas had been harsh and unfriendly toward him before. After this he would be worse. He would never rest until Ross was either dead or safely lodged in jail. He had a personal stake in Ross's capture now. He'd been made to look foolish and feel foolish, and that was something few men could tolerate.

But Ross had gained at least twenty-four hours free of Juan's dogged pursuit. He had to see to it that time wasn't wasted. In that length of time he had to find out who had killed Caine.

First, he had to cover ground. He had to reach Sadie Plue's to-night, get fresh supplies and a fresh horse. He had to be in town at dawn if possible, for only at dawn could he hope to move around as freely as he wished.

He pushed his weary horse as hard as he dared. His face and eyes, in the dark silence of the night, were determined and very grim.

Chapter Ten

Ross Logan knew that in turning back he had, perhaps, doomed himself. The odds against him were mountainous. Had he chosen to do so, he could have put a hundred miles between himself and the sheriff before Mascarenas found another horse. That hundred miles would have meant safety to him. And freedom.

Why had he been so stubborn about turning back? Was it because he wanted to regain the position and respect in the community that he had once enjoyed? Was it because he wanted Horseshoe Ranch? Or was it because of Lily Caine?

The answer wasn't difficult. A position in a community that had so hastily and unjustly condemned was not particularly desirable. Horseshoe Ranch had once been home to him, and was a link with the past, but it was nothing else.

He found his mind dwelling on Lily. He remembered her face, and her eyes, and the way she moved. He knew suddenly that he would do anything to see her again, to hold her in his arms. He would fight for that until he dropped and there must be some chance for him to win.

The answer was here, in the valley of the Horseshoe or in the town of Vail. All he had to do was dig it out.

He smiled faintly to himself as he thought of Juan, plodding along behind him through the night. Juan would walk all night. He'd walk all day to-morrow. Late to-morrow night or early the following day he would reach Sadie Plue's. Unless luck was with him and he happened upon one of her sons tracking wild horses through the badlands.

Juan's temper would be murderous by the time he got another horse. He'd be well aware that only Ross's immediate capture could keep him from becoming the butt of the county's jokes.

Throughout the night as he rode through the rough, dry, barren country of the badlands, Ross searched his mind for answers to the questions that plagued him. But he came up with no better suspect for the murder of Caine than Judge Milburn.

Milburn had to be the one. Unless Caine was killed solely to throw blame on Ross, he was the only one Ross knew of with a good enough reason for killing him.

And it was a powerful reason, if the things Ross believed were true. Milburn's position in the community and his wealth both were at stake. Everything he had schemed and worked for the past fifteen years had been threatened when Caine blackmailed him, further threatened when Ross came home.

Milburn had to be first, then. But what if the judge convinced him he was innocent? Where could he go from there?

However he tried to close his mind against the possibility, a nagging doubt remained. Caine was the type of man who made enemies. There might be a dozen men who had hated him enough to want him dead. And Ross had neither the time nor the knowledge of the people living here now to decide which of Caine's enemies might have finally shot him down.

He urged the grey to greater speed, watching closely for signs of lagging. Twice the grey stumbled, and Ross finally had to let him slow to a walk.

Midnight passed, and as dawn approached, the air grew chill and damp. He stopped to water his horse in Sadie Plue's barn yard, then rode to the door of the house.

It was a big place, but its beginnings were in the single log shack Bert Plue built when he came here with his bride. Rooms had been added on piecemeal as the years went by until the end result was a jumble of assorted constructions and conflicting roof lines. There were at least half a dozen doors opening into the yard.

Ross didn't have to knock. Nor did he dismount. He heard the plain cocking of a rifle and heard Sadie's cracked voice, "Hold it right there, mister, or I'll blow you clear out of your saddle. Who the hell are you and what the hell do you want?"

Ross held himself very still. "It's Ross Logan, Sadie. I need a fresh horse and some grub."

The voice was not so harsh when it came again. "Mascarenas followin' you?"

"Yeah. He's following me. But he's fifty miles west of here afoot."

"He he! Shoot his hoss, did you?" Sadie cackled delightedly as her mind pictured obese Juan Mascarenas plodding bitterly through the night.

"I figured that was the only way I could get the time I need."

"Why you need time? Didn't you kill the son-of-a-bitch?"

"Sorry to disappoint you, but I didn't."

He was silent a moment. Then, with a touch of impatience, he said, "You going to keep me sitting here all night? Or do I get some grub and a horse?"

"You get 'em. Get down an' come on in. Don't reckon I can turn away Tom Logan's son."

He swung from his horse and approached the darkened door. He heard a match strike and a lamp wick flickered. The light strengthened as Sadie lowered the chimney over it.

She turned to face him. She was a tough, bow-legged little woman with a face like the last apple in the barrel in spring. She wore a shapeless flannel nightgown and her grey hair was in untidy braids. But it was the most feminine attire he had ever seen her wear. Usually she wore men's boots, levis, shirt and hat, with her hair tucked up under the crown. She always wore a gun and cartridge belt. She could rope a steer as good as any man.

Still, there must have been something feminine about her once, he thought wryly. She had borne five sons to the man who married her. Ross seemed to remember one daughter who had died in infancy.

She said irritably, "Ain't you never seen a woman in her nightgown before? Quit your starin' at me and fetch some water so I can get the coffee on."

Ross picked up the pail. "Your boys asleep?"

"After all this racket? 'Tain't likely. They'll come stragglin' out here lookin' fer somethin' to eat pretty quick."

Ross went out into the yard and filled the bucket at the pump. He could hear the stove lids rattling in the kitchen and after a moment a cloud of smoke came billowing from the rusty chimney. He carried the water inside.

Sadie was still padding around in bare feet and nightgown. Two of her sons stood at the stove, scratching and rubbing their eyes. Another appeared as Ross went in.

Tall and gangly, they dwarfed their mother, and they had two things in common with each other: A general air of untidyness and hard, direct eyes that looked straight through a man.

The oldest, Luke, had been seven when Bert Prue was killed. Ross glanced at the old woman again, almost furtively. She was tough all right. She'd had to be to raise five sons on a place like this.

The other two appeared. One of these was Luke. He looked closely at Ross as he buttoned a shirt over a hairy belly and growled, "Hear you killed Caine. I guess you know you shot us right out of business. I oughta make you pay for it."

Ross said, "I didn't kill him."

Luke didn't seem to have heard. "An' for a woman too. Ain't they enough women around so's you don't have to kill a man for one?"

Sadie cackled as she dropped huge hunks of meat into a skillet. "Not like this one, mebbe, Luke. Women are like horses. Some's better'n others. I mind the time you'd have killed to get that stud horse down to Junction City."

"Well maybe . . ."

Sadie said, "Besides, Ross says he didn't shoot Caine."

"Then who the hell did?"

Ross watched Luke's face closely. He didn't think any of Sadie's boys were deep enough to avoid showing some guilt if one of them had killed Caine. And Luke's puzzlement seemed genuine.

He experienced a faint, unwilling feeling of disappointment. Besides Judge Milburn, Sadie's boys were the only ones Ross knew who'd had business dealings with Caine. It had occurred to him that one of them might have had reason for killing Caine over some business transaction.

Ross said, "You don't need Caine to sell the horses you catch. Break 'em yourself and sell them to the army direct."

"We don't know all them colonels an' things. There's a lot of fussin' around to it, papers an' such."

"You're as smart as Caine was. You can learn what you need to know. Then you'll make Caine's profit as well as your own."

Again he studied the five surreptitiously, watching for signs that perhaps one of them had thought of this. But they all seemed genuinely surprised, and a bit rueful that they hadn't thought of it themselves.

Outside, the land had turned grey as they talked. The kitchen was warm now, filled with the smell of coffee, frying meat and potatoes. One by one the men went out and ducked their heads under the pump, but none of them shaved.

Ross rubbed the accumulation of whiskers on his face. "Can I borrow a razor from one of you?"

"Sure." Luke went into an adjoining room and returned with a razor, a strop and a shaving brush. Ross took them outside and laid them on a shelf just outside the kitchen door. He got a pan of water and, squinting at himself in the tiny, cracked mirror, scraped his whiskers off.

He went back in, returned the razor to Luke and asked, "Any chance for Mascarenas to get a horse between here and the place I left him last night?"

Luke laughed shortly. "Not a chance. Unless he can catch hisself a wild one to ride."

"And how long would you say it'd take Juan to walk that far?"

"All last night. All to-day and to-night at least. If his feet don't give out. Juan's packin' a slew of lard these days."

Sadie ladled meat and potatoes on to a huge platter and set it down in the centre of the table. The men sat down and began to eat wolfishly. Ross's eyes drooped from not sleeping last night but there was nothing wrong with his appetite.

He glanced around the table at Sadie's sons. He had nothing to fear from them now, for they had no love for the law. But he wondered how it would be if someone were to offer a five hundred dollar reward for him. That might change things considerably. He suddenly felt like a mouse surrounded by hungry cats.

He finished his breakfast and got up from the table. Sadie handed him a gunny sack, half filled and tied at one end. Luke growled, his mouth full of meat, "Take any of them hosses out in the corral that you want. Put your grey in there instead. We'll trade."

Ross nodded. He said, "Thanks, Sadie, for the help."

"Go on, you." She seemed embarrassed by his thanks. He went out, led his horse to the corral, tied him then went inside and roped out the strongest looking one he saw. He changed saddle and bridle, then tied the grub on behind. He mounted, braced for a bucking session.

He was not disappointed, but the horse quit after the first few jumps. Ross raised a hand to Sadie, standing in the door still in nightgown, braids and bare feet, and to her five sons, standing grouped just outside the door.

He received no acknowledgment from them. He rode away, heading straight toward Vail.

If he hurried, he could make it by five o'clock. Some of the townspeople would be up, but most of them would still be inside their houses eating breakfast and getting ready for the day's activities. He spurred the horse, a long-legged bay.

The sun rising, touching the tips of the knolls and hills in the badlands at his back, made him understand why Sadie had been content to live there all her life. It was as beautiful a sight as he had ever seen.

There was a warm glow inside him at the treatment he'd received from Sadie Plue. She didn't give a damn what he'd done, or why. He was Ross Logan, Tom Logan's son and that was enough.

But he knew her sons were different. He had the feeling that any of them would betray him for a ten dollar bill.

Aside from the danger of being ambushed, he doubted if he'd have any trouble in town, even if he was seen. People had a way of taking the view that lawbreakers were strictly the business of the law. And there was no reward for him.

As he rode, with the rising sun beating into his face, he felt a growing anger toward Judge Milburn. If the man was guilty of the things he suspected him of . . . stealing Horseshoe, making a drunk out of Ross's father, killing Caine and seeing that the blame fell on Ross . . .

He had a lot to answer for. Ross suddenly knew he would not be soft when he confronted Milburn this morning at his house. Milburn would talk, or he'd be flat on his back for several days to come. Ross had been pushed as far as he could be pushed. He had nothing to lose by pushing back.

Chapter Eleven

The Horseshoe River ran along the southern border of the town. At this time of year it was still swollen from melting snows in the mountains where it had its source. Wide and deep, it flowed more swiftly than usual, and occasionally carried along a half-submerged log or a cluster of floating sticks and debris.

While he was still a mile from town, Ross put his horse into the river bottom, lower than the surrounding plain, and thick with cottonwoods and brush. This way, he came to the foot of Main Street, where the river was bridged by the road.

He rode under the bridge and continued for about a block. Then he turned his horse into the river and let him wade and swim across. He got his boots full of water and his legs soaked to the knees. But it was better than taking a chance on being seen crossing the bridge.

Prairie, the street a block east of Main, was lined at its lower end with shacks and cheap saloons. A drunk was sleeping comfortably with his back against one of the saloon fronts. A dog was eyeing a cat in the crotch of a tree and trying to pretend indifference.

Except for the soft murmur of the river at his back, the town was quiet. Smoke issued from a few chimneys, but the bulk of the town's inhabitants were still asleep. Ross saw no one on the street but, knowing that noise would attract attention, he rode his horse at a slow walk.

At its upper end, halfway through the town, the character of Prairie Street changed. Trees shaded it here, mostly cottonwoods and elms. The houses became less shabby the farther along he went. He reached Fifth, turned, and a few moments later entered a dusty alley. Half a dozen houses farther on, he stopped behind Judge Milburn's house.

Still sitting his saddle, he looked around, studying the houses around him. No smoke issued from any of their chimneys. He saw no signs to indicate that he was being observed.

He dismounted and led his horse into the judge's stable, where he tied him near the door. Then he emerged and approached the house.

This was the house in which Judge Milburn had been raised. It was a three story frame, Victorian in design, liberally adorned with gables, scroll work at the eaves, and shutters on the windows. Ross rounded the side of it, ducking under the branches of monstrous lilac bushes, and climbed the steps to the front porch.

He raised the brass knocker and let it fall. After several moments, he hammered with it sharply.

He heard a muffled grumbling from inside the house. A moment later the door opened slightly and the judge's face peered out.

Milburn tried desperately to slam the door, but Ross put his shoulder against it and lunged on through. The door slammed back and the judge went sprawling on to the richly carpeted floor.

He was clad in a long, flannel nightshirt that flew up to expose his pale and hairy shanks. His greying hair was tousled and in his eyes was pure terror.

Ross pushed the door shut behind him. He said, "Who else is here?"

"No one." The judge swallowed several times. "My housekeeper's staying with her sister for a couple of days. She doesn't come in until almost noon."

Ross said shortly, "Get up, for Christ's sake. And put on your pants."

Milburn got up. He glanced wildly at the door. Then he headed for the stairs, with Ross following close behind. Ross followed him into his bedroom and waited while he dressed.

The judge's hands shook so violently, he could scarcely manage his clothes. Occasionally he would glance fearfully at Ross.

Once, Ross asked sourly, "What's the matter? Your conscience bad?"

This brought defiance from the judge. "Because I'm scared? Who the hell wouldn't be scared? You've killed two people already."

"You know better than that. You know damned well I haven't killed anybody. Not Ruth and not Caine."

"How would I know?"

"Because *you* killed Caine."

"Why would I kill him? For God's sake, why? He was working for me."

He finished dressing and Ross said harshly, "Go back downstairs."

"What are you going to do? What do you want?"

"Some answers. True ones. And let's get one thing straight right now. I've got nothing to lose. They can't hang me twice."

A muscle in Milburn's face began to twitch violently. He stumbled out into the hall and started down the stairs.

Following closely, Ross frowned to himself. Milburn's terror was too great to be caused just by Ross's appearance here. He knew Ross. He had defended him at his trial. He knew there was no viciousness in him and must know that unless he had something to hide, he had nothing to fear.

It followed, then, that he had something to hide, and while it might be the circumstances surrounding his acquisition of the Horseshoe, it might also be something else.

Milburn went into a book-lined office off the main hall. He collapsed into a chair. He reached into a desk drawer for a cigar.

He seemed to regain some of his composure as he puffed on it. He looked up at Ross, straining for a certain affability. "Are you going to give yourself up, Ross? Do you want me to defend you?"

Ross laughed bitterly. "Like you defended me before? No thanks. Besides, I've got no intention of giving myself up."

"Mascarenas will get you anyway. He's a damned Indian, the way he trails a man."

"He won't get me for a couple of days." He didn't elaborate. If he told Milburn where the sheriff was, Milburn would send out a search party and bring him in. Ross's time would be cut in half.

Ross sat on the corner of the desk. He leaned toward the judge. "Let *me* tell *you* how it was. The markets were bad when I went on trial. Cattle were selling dirt cheap and you were greedy. I was so damned upset at Ruth's death and at being accused of something I hadn't done, that I was in no position to dicker. Neither was Pa. So you told us you'd have to sell Horseshoe to get me off. Then you couldn't find a buyer with the cash money it would take. Times were tough, you said."

Milburn watched him steadily, the affability fading from his eyes.

Ross said, "But you had a little money your father had left you and you could borrow more. You could dig up a dummy buyer for Horseshoe and that was Caine."

Milburn's eyes narrowed slightly. Ross went on, "You sold Horseshoe to him and he sold it back to you. Then you took most of the money you charged for defending me, and paid off what you'd borrowed. What did Horseshoe cost you, actually, besides your time in court? Five hundred? A thousand?"

"Ross, I swear, you've got it wrong.

Caine bought Horseshoe, fair and square. It's not my fault that he didn't do too good with it. He liked horses more than he did cattle. He was always needing money, and I lent it to him. With Horseshoe for security."

"When was your deed recorded, Judge?"

"Ten . . . five years ago."

"I can check the records. I can find out what date was on it and when you recorded it."

Milburn stared up at him a moment. His face seemed to grow flabbier and his body sagged. At last he said, so softly that Ross had to strain to hear, "All right, Ross. I guess you can."

"Then what I've said is true?"

Milburn nodded. "You didn't need Horseshoe. You were going to the pen for fifteen years. You know how few men live to come out after fifteen years. I didn't figure we'd ever see you again."

"What about Pa?"

"He was drinking heavily even before you went to prison. He'd have lost Horseshoe in a couple of years. He didn't care, anyway, after they convicted you."

Ross stared at him with scathing contempt. "That's how you justified it, huh? You needed it more than either of *us* did."

126

Milburn wouldn't look at him. Ross said, "Then Caine started blackmailing you. Threatened to write me at the prison, I suppose. Or threatened to tell Pa. You paid him for a while, and finally he made you let him come and live on Horseshoe since he was supposed to own the place. He broke horses and you ran cattle and everybody was happy for a while. Except Pa, of course. And me."

"I'll make it right, I swear . . ."

"You son-of-a-bitch! I ought to kill you right where you sit!"

"Ross, please . . . !" Milburn was shaking violently.

Ross felt sick at his stomach. With anger and disgust. He said furiously, "How the hell did a weasel like you ever find guts enough to kill a man like Caine?"

"I didn't kill him! I . . ."

Ross's right arm swung viciously. The flat of his hand connected with the side of the judge's face. The chair tipped and the judge sprawled on the floor. Ross glared down at him. "*How* did you kill him? Shoot him in the back?"

"I didn't . . . !"

Ross stepped over the chair and kicked him in the ribs. The judge began to whimper. Ross repeated, "How?"

"I didn't! I didn't! You can kill me, but . . ."

Ross started to kick him again. Then he stopped. Nausea and disgust filled him. He supposed he could beat an admission out of Milburn, but he'd never know whether it was true or whether it was forced out of him, forced because there wasn't enough courage in him to resist.

He experienced discouragement that was almost despair. Milburn had been the best bet he'd had, his most logical suspect for the murder of Caine.

But now he wasn't sure. He looked down at the grovelling, broken man on the floor, realising how little it had taken to break him. How could a thing like this have mustered the courage to kill?

It seemed incredible. Yet he knew that a rat will attack a dog if it is cornered and desperate enough.

He hadn't the stomach for beating Milburn any more. Even if it would have done any good, he couldn't force himself to do it any more.

He said, "Get up!"

Milburn glanced up at him. He read the expressions so plainly written on Ross's face. A deep flush crawled into his own slack face.

He mumbled, "I'll make it right. I swear I will."

"Liar! You'll do everything in your power now to see that I'm caught and hanged. Or killed before I can say anything. But what will you do about Pa? How will you get rid of him? He's your conscience and he'll be around for a long, long time."

"I'll make it right with him."

"Like you've made it right so far? By keeping him soaked with whisky? Or will you try and get rid of him too?"

He stared disgustedly at the judge. This was what a man made of himself when he let greed and pure selfishness rule his life. Milburn had no wife, no family. He lived in this huge, musty mausoleum by himself. Ross would bet his housekeeper was a sour-faced old maid that he probably had hired because she would work cheaper than anybody else.

Milburn struggled to his feet. He stood facing Ross, staring at him fearfully. He thought Ross had sickened of violence, but he could not be sure.

Ross moved suddenly and decisively. His fist slammed out, collided with a sharp crack with the point of Milburn's jaw.

Milburn stumbled back, fell over a chair and collapsed unconscious on the floor.

His mouth was open and saliva drooled from one corner of it.

Ross turned away disgustedly, wiping his knuckles on his pants as though to get dirt off them. He hadn't wanted to touch Milburn, but he hadn't had much choice. He needed time to get safely clear of town. He didn't want an outcry raised the instant he left the judge's house.

This way Milburn would remain unconscious for twenty minutes or so. By that time, Ross could be safely away.

He slammed out of the house, circled it and entered the stable at the rear. Seething with anger and frustration, he mounted and headed north, toward the nearest boundary of the town. It was too late now to ride through it to the river bed, the way he had come in. Too many people were up and around.

He had gone no more than a block when he heard a back door open and close quietly. Glancing around, he saw Phil Rivers hurrying through a weed-grown back yard toward a stable at the rear.

He pulled up abreast of the stable and waited. After a moment, Phil came out, leading his horse. He started violently, then grinned up at Ross sheepishly.

Ross didn't know who lived in the house

Phil had just left, but he did know it wasn't Phil.

Rivers mounted and fell in beside him. He asked, "Isn't it pretty damned risky for you to be in town?"

"No more risky than it is for you to be in that house."

"The husband's gone. Besides . . . well, he's damn' near twice her age." There was a touch of defiance in his eyes.

Ross said, "You don't have to explain to me." There was a moment of awkwardness between them that was finally dispelled by Phil's grin. "Why'd you come back?"

"I went to see the judge."

"Get anything out of him?"

"Not what I wanted. I couldn't get him to admit killing Caine, but I'm pretty sure he did."

"What did he admit?"

"Stealing Horseshoe."

"Well, hell, that's a start, anyway."

Ross nodded, frowning faintly. The old, easy relationship he'd once had with Phil seemed to be gone. He said, "We never did get to have that talk. Juan broke it up. Why don't you ride along with me for a ways?"

"I'd like to. But I've got to get home."

"You married?"

Phil shook his head, but he didn't speak.

Ross felt a sense of frustration. Still trying to recapture the old closeness, he asked, "What are you doing these days? Still have that piece of land up north?"

"Huh-uh. Sold it. I'm a cattle trader now. Buy 'em and ship 'em east. I was out on a buying trip when you got back. I'd just gotten home when I ran into you in the saloon."

He halted his horse. "I've got to turn back. You need any money or anything, Ross?"

Ross shook his head. Phil said, "See you, then. Take care. Juan's a damned bloodhound."

Ross nodded. He watched Phil ride away, lingering until Phil turned a corner and disappeared.

Frowning to himself, he continued toward the edge of town. Phil was heavier than Ross remembered him. Growing fleshy, and slightly bald. He supposed it was normal that fifteen years would destroy the closeness there had once been between them. He used to be able to guess what Phil was thinking, but he couldn't any more. Common interests were gone.

But Phil was still a loyal friend. Nothing could change that.

A boy of about fifteen was driving a cow in across a fenced pasture toward a house at the very edge of town. The boy's dog rushed to Ross and barked, but Ross didn't know whether the boy could recognise him or not.

It didn't matter particularly if he did. When Milburn came to, the town would know he'd been here anyway.

He rode straight north for about a mile until he was hidden by a rise of land. Then he turned east.

His mind kept remembering his early years here, and some of the times he'd had with Phil. His mouth twisted into a wry grin as he remembered the incident of the buck deer getting up and running, with him clinging to the animal's back and Phil standing there in the brush roaring with laughter and shouting ribald encouragement.

He recalled other times — the dances at the Odd Fellows Hall, some of the fights when Phil and he stood back to back slugging it out with all comers and enjoying every minute of it.

Too bad that nothing endured. Phil had changed. But then so had he.

Well clear of the town, he turned south and lined his horse out on a course that headed toward Horseshoe and toward Vail's ranch beyond.

Chapter Twelve

Ross wished, as he rode, that he knew the circumstances surrounding Caine's murder, If he knew how Caine had been killed, and where, he would be in a much better position to decide how good a suspect Judge Milburn was.

It was hard to believe that such a snivelling coward could ever have pulled the trigger against a man like Caine. Yet so far, Milburn was the only one he knew of with a reason for killing Caine.

Frowning, he asked himself what he did know about Caine's death. Caine must have been killed at night, and he must have been killed in town. And if he had been shot from behind, Milburn could still be a suspect after all.

Ross grinned faintly to himself as his mind pictured the judge's actions when he first revived. The grin widened briefly, then faded and went away. There would probably be a reward out for him before the day was through. Judge Milburn would see to that. And a reward wouldn't help his chances much.

Furthermore, proving fraud in the sale of Horseshoe fifteen years ago was going to be difficult, with the only witness dead. The mere fact that deeds had been recorded, first in Caine's name and later in Judge Milburn's, proved nothing. No fraud at least. So Milburn's admissions to him earlier did him little good.

Time seemed to be pressing in on him. There remained to him only to-day, and possibly to-night, and then Mascarenas would be on his trail again, vengeful and more determined than before.

He rode steadily as the sun mounted in the eastern sky. He crossed the boundary of Horseshoe, debating whether to stop or not. He finally decided he would, and admitted that the main thing influencing his decision was growing doubt that he would get another chance.

Of one thing he was sure. They weren't going to take him alive. He had seen the last of prison bars. He had not killed Ruth, or Caine. He had killed only once in his entire life and that in self-defence. But he would kill. He'd kill Juan Mascarenas or anyone else that tried to capture him.

The sun grew hot. Clouds began to form miles to the west, beyond the badlands where Sadie Plue lived with her sons. In mid-morning, Ross saw the familiar buildings of Horseshoe ahead.

He stopped while yet half a mile away, and studied the place carefully. Lily was out in the yard hanging clothes. A single horse drowsed, head down, in the corral. A few white chickens scratched busily in the dust before the barn.

Though she was too far away to see clearly, her face, her features, her eyes were suddenly very plain in his mind.

He touched his horse's sides with the spurs and thundered toward the house. She looked up when she heard the pound of his horse's hoofs, her face white, her eyes wide.

She was holding a piece of laundry just taken from the basket. She dropped it into the dust and ran toward him, holding up her skirts so that she would not trip.

From a distance of fifty feet he could see her tears, her terror, her relief that he was alive and safe. Then he was on the ground, and hurrying toward her too.

She was in his arms. There was no hesitation now, no holding back. Her body shook violently and tears continued to stream across her cheeks.

He held her hard against his chest until her trembling began to subside, sometimes stroking her smooth hair with his hand. Then he held her away from him and searched her face hungrily.

Her words came in a torrent, as her tears had done. "Are you all right, Ross? You look so thin, so tired. Are you hungry? Where is the sheriff and the posse? Are they close behind you? Why didn't you go . . . Oh, why didn't you leave?"

"Did you want me to?"

"I told you . . . I would have . . . Oh, Ross, I'm so glad you're all right! I've been worried . . . I couldn't sleep . . ."

Ross said, "I shot Juan's horse over in the badlands, and the last I saw of him he had nearly fifty miles to walk. So I'm safe for to-day, and for to-night too, probably. Come on, let's go to the house."

"Are you hungry?"

He shook his head. "I had breakfast at Sadie Plue's. She gave me a sack of grub and a fresh horse. I've just come from town."

She brushed hastily at her eyes to clear away the tears. She smiled, and it was like watching the sun come out after a thunderstorm.

He picked up his horse's reins. Lily hugged his arm close against her as they walked toward the house. Her eyes rested steadily on his face, as though she too believed this was the last time she would see him alive.

He wanted her, and he knew she would give herself to him; yet he knew it was unfair and he couldn't ask it. The closer they became, the more it would hurt her if something happened to him.

They reached the house. He tied his horse and followed her inside. She stood in the centre of the kitchen, her eyes steady, trusting and warm.

Knowing that if the silence wasn't broken by something ordinary, he'd do what he'd promised himself he wouldn't do, he asked, "Got any coffee?"

"Of course. Sit down and I'll get you a cup."

He sat down at the table. Lily's hands were trembling as she put a cup in front of him. They trembled as she poured the coffee, so badly that she spilled some beside the cup.

Her eyes never left his face. He said, "I saw Judge Milburn in town a while ago. I think he killed your husband, but I couldn't get him to admit anything. He did admit stealing Horseshoe fifteen years ago, though." His mouth twisted wryly. "Not that it will do me any good. Caine was the only one who could have made a case against him stick. All Milburn has to do is deny everything. The deeds and the way they were recorded don't prove anything. Even if both deeds were dated the same day, it isn't enough to recover Horseshoe and send Milburn to jail."

"Where are you going now?"

He forced himself to look away from her. With his eyes on her face, on her full warm mouth, it was difficult for him to think of anything but her. He shrugged. "Vail's place, I guess. If I could find out who killed Ruth fifteen years ago it might help. Then maybe somebody would believe me when I said I didn't kill Caine."

"Will I see you again, soon?"

He nodded, gulped the last of the coffee and got to his feet, knowing that his chances of ever seeing her again were slim. He took her in his arms, lowered his head and kissed her on the mouth. He pulled away almost violently and went to the door.

He stepped out into the bright sunshine and Lily followed him. He looked at the laundry she had been hanging, and at the piece she had dropped in the dust. He said, "You dropped one. You'll have to do it over."

"Yes, I suppose I will. It doesn't matter . . ."

It was a meaningless conversation, the words said only to avoid saying the things uppermost in both their minds.

Ross untied his horse and mounted. "Good-bye, Lily."

"Good-bye, Ross."

He said, "It doesn't look too good right now, but I'll make it come out all right. I'll come back."

"Yes, Ross. Of course you will."

He swung his horse abruptly and rode out of the yard at a gallop. He looked back once and raised his hand, but Lily didn't see. She was sitting on the stoop, her face buried in her hands, her shoulders shaking with weeping.

Frowning, Ross went on. There had been despair in the way Lily wept. But instead of discouraging him, it made him more determined and fed the anger that smouldered in his mind.

He scowled as he rode toward Vail's ranch. No puzzle was without a solution and this was no exception. Somewhere there was an answer to it. And somehow he would find that answer.

He rode cautiously as he crossed Vail's land and it was well that he did. Halfway there he saw three of Vail's riders approaching him.

Seething at the delay, he concealed himself in a deep wash and watched as they drew closer, came abreast and passed on. His horse, catching the scent of theirs, nickered softly and would have done so again had not Ross clamped a sudden hand over his nostrils.

The men went on, talking, laughing, and when they were only specks in the distance, Ross came out of the wash and continued toward Vail's ranch.

How he would get to Vail, in daylight, in his own ranch house, he didn't know. But he couldn't wait for night. He couldn't waste that much time.

Vail's ranch house was an enormous, two-story log building, thirty or forty years old. It was surrounded by ten or twelve other buildings, ranging in size from the barn, which dwarfed even the house, to the tiny ice house nestled snugly in a grove of cottonwoods.

There were horses in the corral, and men moving about the yard. Ross stopped his horse and studied the place doubtfully.

A large spring came out of the ground near Vail's house, filled the troughs in the corrals, and continued toward Ross along a shallow draw. He could see where the water petered out because that was where the trees, brush and vegetation also petered out. Along that brushy draw was the route by which Ross would have to approach the place. And he'd have to do it afoot, taking his chances that he could get in and out unobserved.

Accordingly, he rode to the draw, entered the grove of trees, and rode concealed for as far as he dared. Dismounting, he tied his horse and continued on foot.

Voices came to him now, and the normal daytime sounds of a busy ranch. He wondered if Vail was here. If he wasn't . . .

But he was committed, and besides there was no place else he could go. Vail was the only one he could think of who might have been implicated in Ruth's death.

Vail's protestations that he had thought highly of her meant nothing, Ross realized. Perhaps he *had* thought highly of her at first. But if he'd ever found out what she really was . . . Ross knew that the anger of a man like Vail could be mountainous.

Fortunately, on this side of the house there was practically no activity. Ross glanced up at the sun. It was getting close to noon . . . to the time when Vail's men would be quitting for dinner.

He hurried after he realised that. Breathless, he came up on the shady north wall of the house unobserved.

Cutting a screen and entering an open window presented no difficulties. And he found himself standing inside the house, in Vail's own office, untidy and cluttered, but somehow businesslike for all of that.

He crossed the room to the door, opened it and peered into the hall. From the direction of the kitchen came the sounds of meal preparations and the smell of frying meat. From the other direction there was only silence.

Ross stepped into the hall and walked quickly to its end. He looked out into the enormous living-room, and saw the back of Vail's head showing above the back of one of the leather-covered chairs.

Swiftly he crossed the room. Drawing his gun, he put its muzzle against Vail's neck.

"Don't yell, and don't make any sudden moves. I want to talk to you."

Vail started to turn his head, stopped as Ross pushed the gun muzzle harder against his neck. Ross could see the flush of fury that crept into his face. Vail's voice was choked as he asked, "What the hell do *you* want?"

"Talk. Get up real slow and walk down that hall to your office. We'll talk in there."

"Like hell . . ." Vail swung his head and looked at Ross. He got up unwillingly and walked down the hall ahead of Ross. Ross stepped into the office behind him and closed the door.

He breathed a long, slow sigh of relief. He had succeeded thus far, and it was more than he'd had any right to expect. He had entered Vail's house without being seen and he had managed to get Vail in here.

Vail's face was still flushed dangerously. He said harshly, "How far do you think you're going to get when you leave this place?"

Ross shrugged. "I got away from Juan's posse and I got away from Juan. Maybe I can get away from you too."

"What do you want? Why come here?"

"Because I think you know something about Ruth's death. Because I'm going to have some answers before I leave."

Chapter Thirteen

For several moments Vail stared at him unbelievingly. Arrogance came naturally to Vail and his expression was arrogant now. He shouted, "You think I know something about it? Why goddam you, Logan, I . . ."

Ross said evenly, "Keep your voice down."

Vail stared at him truculently.

Ross said, "If you'll admit for a moment that maybe I didn't kill her after all, then you'll have to admit something else. Someone did. And they haven't paid for it."

He studied Vail closely as he spoke, surprised to find the man studying him with equal closeness. For a second time to-day, Ross felt discouragement. This was turning into another blind canyon. Vail might be many things but he wasn't devious. He couldn't have feigned this kind of outrage and he couldn't have met Ross's eyes so steadily if he'd been responsible for Ruth's death and for Ross's imprisonment.

Ross said, "Let's talk about it. Try and remember all you can. How many times did you see Ruth in all?"

Vail was silent for several moments, watching Ross defiantly. It was plain that he resented another man's intrusion into his memories. It was also plain that he didn't intend to share them with anyone.

Ross asked softly, "Do you want her killer running free?"

"You . . . How do I know . . . ?"

Ross said, "You don't. But you're wondering, aren't you?" He was virtually certain now that Vail wasn't implicated in Ruth's death. But maybe he knew something, something that would point the way. If he didn't there would be nothing further Ross could do. He'd have used up all his ideas. Ross said, "Think back. How many times did you see her?"

"Half a dozen maybe." Even after all these years, it still plainly hurt Vail to think of Ruth. He had really been in love with her, thought Ross. And it had been a silent kind of love that asks nothing in return. Foolish for a man as earthy as Vail, perhaps, but admirable in its way as any unselfishness is admirable.

"When was the first?"

"The day you brought her from Kansas City."

"And the next?"

"A month later, maybe." Vail had no trouble remembering. He must have gone over each time he'd seen Ruth a thousand times in his mind.

"Where was she?"

"In town. I was standing in front of the store when she drove up. I helped her down from her buggy."

Vail was flushing now, partly with embarrassment, partly with anger at his own discomfiture. Ross thought wryly that he had probably been flushing as painfully when he helped Ruth down from her buggy. And she had known instantly that Vail . . .

He asked, "What did she say to you?"

"Thanked me. Invited me to come out to Horseshoe."

"That all?"

Vail nodded.

"And you went out to Horseshoe to see her?"

Vail nodded again. "Several times. You were there once, but I don't suppose you remember it. I knew it was wrong, but I kept making excuses to myself." Vail glanced up, met Ross's eyes, and for the first time there was no condemnation in them. Not for Ross at least. He said, as though with some surprise, "Maybe I was too ready to believe you did it. Maybe I wanted to blame you so I wouldn't feel so damned guilty myself."

Ross clenched his jaws. Vail had cherished these memories so long that it was doubtful if he remembered anything connected with them that did not actually concern Ruth. He had to be jolted out of their rosy glow if he was going to do Ross any good.

Ross said brutally, "And then one day you caught someone with her. Who was it? And when you did, it ruined that pretty, untouchable image you'd created in your mind, didn't it? But why didn't you kill the man? Why did you have to come back and kill Ruth?"

Vail lunged at him, eyes wild, face contorted. "Liar! You dirty, stinkin' liar! I never . . ."

Ross caught his wrists and held him ruthlessly. Their faces inches away, they glared at each other.

Ross whispered savagely, "Why'd you stop? Who did you remember?"

"Nobody, damn you! Nobody that had anything to do with her."

A terrible intensity was in Ross's voice. "Who? You son-of-a-bitch, tell me!"

"Rivers. Phil Rivers. I ran into him a couple of times riding away from your place. But he was your friend. Hell, I didn't think anything about it. And you're wrong, anyway. You're wrong! She wouldn't . . . not with your best friend!"

Ross looked at him pityingly. He said, "You're a fool! A stupid, blind fool. You still think she was an angel, don't you? But she wasn't! She even tried to get my own father . . . !"

He didn't get to finish that. Vail, with strength that was almost superhuman, broke savagely away from him. Like an animal, Vail attacked him, arms windmilling with his fury, and bore him back across the room.

Off balance, at a disadvantage, Ross knew instantly that he couldn't afford a bruising fight with Vail. Not here. It would bring Vail's crew running.

With his back against the wall, with Vail's fists pummelling blindly, Ross drew his gun. He brought it up and clipped Vail on the top of the head with its long barrel. Vail went to his knees, only partly conscious, and Ross stepped away.

Vail stared up at him, hatred undiminished in his eyes. He might doubt that Ross had killed Ruth physically, but he hated him now for another, stronger reason. Ross had killed the image of purity he had carried so long in his mind.

But Ross had what he'd come here for. He knew something at last, something . . . after all these years.

He stepped hurriedly across the room and climbed out the window to the ground beneath. As he did, he heard running footsteps in the hall.

Bending low, he ran for the cover of brush and trees in the tiny draw.

Behind him he heard voices, a shout, the tinkle of glass breaking. A shot cracked, and another, and then he was in the brush and running to reach his horse ahead of their pursuit.

How long it would take them to get organised, he couldn't tell. But get organised they would. And leading them, more vengeful and furious than Mascarenas could ever be, would be Vail himself.

Ross reached his horse, mounted, whirled him and spurred savagely away. He broke from the trees and brush at the end of the draw on a dead run and kept the horse travelling that way for a couple of miles.

He felt angry and helpless and somehow unclean. Digging into the past, searching for Ruth's killer, was like rooting around in garbage searching for tiny bits of truth that would also turn out to be garbage when they were found.

Like what he had discovered about Phil. His face twisted involuntarily.

Considering it, though, considering what he knew about Phil, he realised that friendship had blinded him. Phil had never been very responsible. It was part of what made him so likeable. And he'd always had a way with women, who found that very irresponsibility irresistible.

Seeing Phil clearly for the first time, Ross realised something else. Phil's loyalty had slipped a number of times over the years. And each time it had, a woman had been involved.

But he should have guessed a long time ago. He should have guessed. Vail had met Phil leaving Horseshoe twice. And Vail had only been out there three or four times. Phil must have seen an awful lot of Ruth. Maybe he'd gotten tired of her and told her he wasn't coming back.

Something like that would have been hard for Ruth to take. She'd probably tried to hold him by threatening to tell Ross about their relationship.

Scowling, Ross wondered why his father hadn't known about Phil and Ruth. But he knew the answer to that almost immediately. His father had been staying away from Horseshoe himself, deliberately. He'd been avoiding Ruth, seeing as little of her as he could. Because she had tried . . . because she had made him want her and because, perhaps, he couldn't trust himself.

A devil, she had been. She had deserved to die. Living, she had left a wake of men broken by guilt and shame. Even in death, she had been able to destroy.

At each rise of ground, Ross swung around in his saddle and stared behind. He was nearly five miles from Vail's place, however, before he saw the dust of the pursuit.

His mind seethed with fury as he thought of Rivers, sneaking out to Horseshoe, making love to Ruth in spite of the fact that he was Ross's friend. And then, worse, killing her and being too cowardly to take the punishment for it, letting Ross take the punishment instead.

Fifteen years. Fifteen years of his life. Horseshoe . . .

His jaws clenched, his eyes like iron, Ross forced the horse to run at breakneck speed, taking everything the horse had to give. Somehow he had to outdistance Vail and his men, lose them. Somehow he had to get to town, and get his hands on Phil.

He veered east and after several miles saw the pursuit turn east along the trail he had made. He angled south, and they clung to his trail stubbornly and determinedly.

He tried to recall what the horse in Lily Caine's corral had been like. Had the animal been young, and strong? He cursed softly because he couldn't remember even noticing the horse. But he'd need a fresh one. He'd have to take everything this one had, and wear those of Vail's men down. He'd have to reach Horseshoe before his own horse dropped, then head out for town on the fresh one Lily had kept in her corral.

Pondering it, he was willing to bet the horse she had kept up was both young and strong. Furthermore, he was almost certain she had kept the horse in for only one reason. She had kept him in the corral for Ross when he needed a fresh mount.

Impossible to lose pursuit on the open plain . . . but he could make them follow trail, and could thus gain ground.

Thereafter he kept to the long, wide,

shallow draws and avoided the ridge tops where they might spot him in spite of the distance between. Still he rode at top speed, but briefly now and then he would slow the horse to a trot.

The horse was lathered heavily. Flecks of foam blew from his mouth and from his neck. His lungs worked like a gigantic bellows.

Inevitably, he began to falter. He stumbled often. Reluctantly, Ross slowed him to a walk and turned his head toward Horseshoe Ranch. This horse was done.

But he had served Ross well. The pursuit was now at least half a dozen miles behind, riding worn-out horses just as Ross was. On the fresh horse in Lily's corral, he could reach town far enough ahead of them to finish his business with Rivers and be away again before they could arrive.

His business with Rivers. Anger churned in his thoughts. Not only had Rivers betrayed him fifteen years ago with Ruth; he had let Ross serve fifteen years in prison for killing her.

What kind of man could do those things and still eat, and sleep, and do the thousand things that make up a normal life? Conscience had turned Ross's father into a drunk. Conscience had troubled even Orv

Milburn to the extent that he had cared for Tom Logan's needs. But what effect had Phil Rivers' conscience had? None, apparently. He had gained weight. He seemed the same untroubled man he had always been. He had been able to greet Ross in the saloon a couple of nights ago as though nothing were amiss.

Could his suspicions of Phil be wrong, he wondered uneasily.

He forced the horse into a trot. Getting to town, seeing Rivers — these things were suddenly more important to him than anything else.

It was mid-afternoon before he saw the buildings at Horseshoe ahead of him. Lily was in the yard. He saw her shade her eyes against the sun and peer at him in the distance.

Then, lifting her skirts, she ran across to the corral. She went in.

He saw the horse plunging, running. He saw her following, her skirts frightening the horse.

Though the horse he was riding was completely exhausted, he sank his spurs and forced the animal into a faltering gallop. The distance between him and the ranch slowly closed.

Lily was having no luck, but she was

155

trying. She had recognised him and she was trying to catch the half-wild horse and have him saddled by the time Ross arrived.

He reached the corral. His horse stopped and stood, head down, wheezing painfully.

Lily lay on her back in the centre of the corral. Ross slammed open the gate, went in and gathered her up in his arms.

He carried her outside, kicked the gate shut behind him. He laid her down and ran for the pump.

Returning, he bathed the nasty-looking lump on her forehead with cold water from the well. She opened her eyes.

There was terror in them briefly as they went beyond Ross. When she realised he was alone, the terror left them and they filled with tears. "I wanted to have him all saddled and ready for you. I tried . . . but he was afraid of my skirts, I guess. He kicked . . ."

"It's all right. Don't worry about it. How do you feel?"

She struggled to sit up. She smiled wanly. "I've a headache. But don't worry about me." She glanced at his horse and the fear returned instantly to her eyes. "Someone's after you! Oh, Ross!"

He kissed the bruise on her forehead gently. "I've got a minute."

Her words came tumbling out frantically. "You've got to get away! You've got to leave now! Judge Milburn has posted a five thousand dollar reward for you, dead or alive. Everyone in town, most everyone at least, is out riding around looking for you. They won't risk trying to take you alive. They'll shoot . . ."

"They'll have to," he said grimly.

"Go away, Ross, now! Leave the county. I'll come wherever you want me to, whenever you let me know." Tears of cold fear filled her eyes again. "Please, Ross. Please! I'm so afraid for you!"

He put his arms around her, awkwardly because of their positions on the ground. He held her hard against his chest.

She was offering him so much and all he had to do was go away. He could feel her warmth, her softness, her strength. There was promise in the future for him for the first time in many years. All he had to do was agree. All he had to do was mount that horse in there and go. He still had time to get clear, to escape.

He said, "To-morrow, Lily. To-morrow. I've got to see Phil Rivers first and then I'll go."

"You can't go to town! Not with that reward! Every man in town . . ."

"I've got to, Lily. I've got to!"

She pulled away and looked up into his face. She said softly, "Yes. But promise me that to-morrow . . . if you're still free . . ."

He nodded, "I promise. After I've seen Phil, there will be nothing more that I can do." The look in her brimming eyes made him say, "It will be better staying here, Lily. Better than running and hiding all our lives. It's worth this one last chance."

She nodded wordlessly, but he could see she didn't agree. He lifted her to her feet. "Sure you're all right?"

Smiling faintly she leaned against the corral fence. "A little dizzy. But all right."

He went into the corral and roped the horse. He could feel her eyes resting on him all that time. When he had saddled the animal and faced her again, he could see only thankfulness in her that she had seen him once more, and a despairing belief that she would not see him again.

He seized her in his arms. There was hunger in him now, and need. But most of all there was a compulsion to make her believe that he still had a chance.

He was a rabbit, surrounded by a pack of dogs. But in spite of that . . . He swung to the horse's back.

Looking down at her, he saw a new expression in her face that puzzled him. Firmness. Almost determination. But there was no more time. He could see the dust raised by Vail and his riders, now less than two miles away. He could see the riders themselves.

"To-morrow, Lily. I promise, to-morrow." He whirled the horse and sank his spurs. He thundered out of the yard in the direction of town.

Looking back, he saw her throwing a saddle onto his worn-out horse. As he watched, she mounted and followed him.

Cursing softly, he whirled his horse. It had suddenly become very important to him to know what she was intending to do. His mind could only remember the firmness and determination that had been in her face as he rode away.

Chapter Fourteen

He reached her in less than a minute, and reined his plunging horse to a halt facing her. He raised his eyes and glanced past her at the rapidly approaching riders.

Then he looked at her face. "Where are *you* going?"

"Ross, they're almost here. You can't stay. They'll . . ."

"I'm not going until you tell me what you're up to."

Her face held a hesitant, fearful, but nevertheless determined expression. She said, "I'm going into town. Is anything wrong with that?"

"From the look in your face there is. What . . ." He could hear the pound of approaching hoofs now, like a rumble travelling through the ground. They'd be close enough to use their rifles soon.

Lily also heard. Terror touched her face, and defeat came to her eyes. They filmed with tears. She cried, "I'll go back, if you'll go on. Please, Ross!"

"What . . . ?"

"Oh all right. I was going into town and tell them I'd killed my husband. I thought if you had a little more time . . ."

Ross stared at her for the briefest instant. Then he said softly, "Go back, Lily."

She nodded numbly. Ross whirled his horse and galloped away, at right angles to the course he would normally take toward town. A rifle cracked among the oncoming horsemen, and another. Dust kicked up a dozen yards behind him.

Knowing that Lily was now out of the line of fire, he swerved directly toward town. He glanced back, at the pursuing horsemen with Vail leading them, and at Lily, sitting frozen on her worn-out horse. Then he sank his spurs, leaning forward over the horse's withers, and rode.

The distance began to widen almost immediately. In ten minutes he was leading them by half a mile.

He didn't slacken pace. But his thoughts were concerned with Lily now, rather than with Vail and his men.

He wondered if she understood how dangerous was the thing she had meant to do. People had been convicted of murder on less evidence than she had intended to provide. If she had surrendered herself — and if Ross had subsequently been killed — she would undoubtedly have gone to prison at the very least.

Then he remembered the fear that had been in her face. She had understood fully the consequences of what she had planned, he realized. And she would have gone through it to take the pressure off him or to give him time to get away.

A rare and wonderful woman, he thought. A woman who, committing herself, did so fully and without reservation.

Conflicting emotions stirred in him. He felt humility, to be the recipient of such a love. He felt a stronger love for her himself than he had felt before. He felt also a compelling desire to live, to come back to her. And he felt rising anger at his own helplessness, at the fact that but one chance of clearing himself remained.

The miles flowed steadily behind. He was leading Vail and his men now by several miles.

But his time was limited, even after he reached the town. It was limited to the time that would be required for Vail to reach it and locate him.

With that kind of reward out for him . . . He admitted that his chances of even reaching Phil Rivers's house weren't very good.

The sun sank steadily in the west. It had been down almost five minutes when Ross thundered across the bridge and up the dusty street.

The light dusk that lay across the land — the time of day when everyone was normally finishing supper — helped him now. He saw only half a dozen people on the street, all of them at least a block beyond the first intersection.

He slowed his horse to a sedate trot, knowing that nothing would draw attention to him quicker than a breakneck pace. Watchfully he rode, his eyes glancing warily to right and left.

Five thousand dollars was a tremendous amount of money. It was enough to set a man up with a good ranch and a herd of cattle. It would buy half a dozen houses, or almost any business establishment in town. It was enough to make nine out of any ten men risk their lives. It was enough to dissipate most men's principles.

Judge Milburn had purposely made it high, he thought. The higher the reward the better the chance that it would be collected for him dead rather than alive.

Ross started violently as a hoarse shout

broke the stillness of the tree-shaded street. He swung his head.

A shot racketed and the bullet thudded into a tree ten feet to his right. He saw a middle-aged man half a block back in the direction he had come levering another shell into his rifle and resting it against the trunk of a tree for a better shot.

He reined his horse to the left violently and sank his spurs. The animal plunged across a lawn, cleared a white picket fence and thundered across a back yard to the alley beyond.

The shot, he thought bitterly, would alert the whole damned town. It would draw men from their homes, weapons in their hands. It would make him a target all the way to Rivers's house.

He'd have to leave his horse. He had no other choice. On horseback, he'd be unmistakable.

And this would slow him disastrously. Vail and his crew must be almost to town by now. With them combing it, with the townsmen searching for him . . .

He swung from the running horse's back and led the animal into a small shed. Hastily he tied the reins, hoping the horse would still be there when he returned. If the horse was found . . . if he was removed from this shed . . . then Ross would be finished. Afoot in a town as hostile as this, without a horse on which to escape.

His jaws firmed out. Damn them. They weren't going to stop him this close to Phil Rivers's house. They weren't going to cheat him of this one last chance to clear himself.

He glanced up and down the alley as he left the shed. He could hear the man who had shot at him shouting to others back there in the street. Their voices were closer. The man yelled, "Go up to the end of the alley and cut him off. Remember, whoever gets him, half the reward is mine. I saw him first!"

Ross's face was grim. He wasn't a man to them any more. He was five thousand dollars. He was no better than an animal — a wolf — upon which the bounty was exorbitantly high.

He left the alley and cut through another yard, travelling slowly and silently. Rounding the corner of the house, he startled a woman, who screamed shrilly.

He reversed directions, leaping fences, crashing through piles of trash and tin cans, then crossed another yard and so reached the street.

Five riders thundered past as Ross concealed himself behind the trunk of a giant cottonwood. His gun in his hand, loosely held but ready.

He raced across the street as soon as the horsemen disappeared into the dusk. A dog barked at him and ran after him, nipping at his heels.

An equal danger to him at the moment, he realised, equal to that of being killed or captured was that, coming face to face with a townsman intent on killing him, he would kill in defence of his life.

Then he would truly be a murderer. And there would be no clearing himself, now or ever again.

He cursed the dog as the animal seized the leg of his pants. The gun descended, its barrel striking the dog's head. The animal fell, lying on his side on the ground, but twitching as though he were dreaming.

Ross plunged through another yard and raced up the alley to its end.

He halted there and glanced into the street. Behind him rose sounds of the search, but it seemed to be centred back there a block away from him.

Three men ran across the alley mouth, guns in their hands, without seeing him. Walking, he crossed the street to the alley beyond.

Two shots cracked out in the direction the men had been travelling. Ross smiled ruefully. They were shooting at each other now. And that was dangerous for him too. Because if anyone was hit, rather than take the blame for being stupid and trigger-happy, the shooter would probably lay the blame on Ross.

He'd better get to Phil's house, see him and then get the hell out of town. It had probably been foolish to come here in the first place. He should have known.

He travelled a whole block without seeing anyone. And then, so suddenly it took him by surprise, he saw Phil Rivers's house looming ahead of him.

The sky was now almost completely dark. But no lamplight winked from the windows here.

His first reaction was one of disappointment. Risking his neck, riding into this hornet's nest had been useless.

But as he stood there staring at the house he felt an almost animal sense of danger, of warning, of menace. And things began to click neatly into place.

Vail was in town with his men. Ross had seen three of them galloping along the street. Phil could hardly have failed to hear the commotion.

Why wasn't it possible that Phil had talked to Vail or to one of Vail's men? It was possible, Ross realised. It was even probable. And if Phil had talked to Vail, then he knew Ross was hunting him.

His mouth twisted faintly in the darkness. He approached the house silently.

Eagerness was in him now. He was close to the answer that had tormented him all during the past fifteen years. Phil was here, he knew instinctively. Phil was waiting up there in the house, probably with a gun in his hand.

Phil would, if his suspicions of the man were correct, shoot him as quickly as anyone else in town. So he'd have to be careful.

He reached the porch and stepped cautiously upon it. It creaked thunderously. Ross flung himself back, rolling frantically though the high grass immediately in front of it.

Instantly he hit the ground he knew he had walked into a trap. For a full ten seconds it sounded like an Indian battle in front of Rivers's house. Shots blasted at him from both front windows and from the door. There must have been half a dozen guns.

Ross clawed along the grass desperately,

trying to reach the doubtful shelter of a bush. Bullets continued to tear into the porch, into the columns supporting the porch roof, and into the ground immediately in front of it.

Though Ross's gun was in his hand, he didn't use it. They couldn't see him now, and it would be foolish to reveal his location to them.

Vail's men, he supposed. And Vail. The man had known Ross would head directly here after the things that had been said out at his ranch earlier this afternoon.

He heard a hoarse shout. "Les, get a lamp. We must've got the bastard."

That voice . . . he'd know it anywhere. It didn't belong to Vail or to any of his men. It belonged to Luke Plue, Sadie's oldest son. Les was one of his brothers. Hell, they all must be here.

No wonder it had sounded like a war as they opened up on him. And if he didn't get out of here . . .

He eased carefully back from the bush behind which he'd taken cover. As soon as he dared, he got to his feet and ran.

Light flickered alive back there. Phil Rivers and Sadie's five sons emerged cautiously from the house. They began to search the yard and the shrubbery.

From the centre of town more men were coming. Ross ducked behind a tree and allowed four of them to pass.

They were talking excitedly, out of breath from running.

Good God Almighty, he thought, this was a Roman holiday. They were hunting him the way a bunch of boys will hunt a rat — respectful of his sharp teeth but aware too how small and outnumbered he is.

The presence of Sadie's sons at Rivers's house bothered him. There hadn't been time . . . they couldn't have known about the talk he'd had with Vail or about what was said.

Only one conclusion remained, and accepting it made him feel a little sick. The Plues had heard about the reward. They'd come to town, not because they'd thought Ross would be here, but because they'd figured Phil Rivers to be the one most likely to know where Ross could be found. They'd teamed up with him, and probably had agreed on a split of the reward.

The fact that the house had been dark . . . the fact that all six of them had opened up on him . . . led to but one additional conclusion. Rivers had agreed. He had agreed to help them kill or capture Ross.

But there was no reason for Ross to be surprised. If his suspicions were correct, Rivers had never been his friend. He had betrayed him twice, fifteen years ago. The first time with Ruth. The second when he allowed Ross to go to prison for the crime of killing her.

Angry, baffled cries rose into the air a block behind. They hadn't found him. They'd found no blood. They knew he had escaped.

He smiled grimly to himself, thinking how terrified Phil Rivers now must be.

It pleased him to think of Rivers shivering in his boots. Let him shiver, damn him. The time was coming . . .

He hadn't had an opportunity to talk to Phil. He hadn't been able to wring the truth from him.

But the dangerous trip to town was not altogether a failure in spite of that. He *knew*, as surely as if Phil had confessed to him. Phil had killed Ruth.

Now all he had to do was convince Juan Mascarenas that Phil was the guilty one.

All he had to do. He shook his head grimly. That might be the most difficult thing he had tried to do so far.

Chapter Fifteen

The search for him was centred in the immediate vicinity of Phil Rivers's house. But it was spreading out. He retraced the route he had travelled earlier and got to within half a block of his horse before a group of men discovered him.

Fortunately they were mounted. He raced ahead of them through two yards, over fences their horses could not or would not clear in the dark, then doubled back toward the shed where he had left his horse.

He ducked into the shed, untied his horse and mounted. He rode into the alley and along it to its end.

Coming out of the alley mouth, he ran into two of the three who had been pursuing him earlier. One of them yelled, "See him, Jack?"

Ross grunted, "Huh-uh," and let his horse fall in at the rear of theirs. Sooner or later Jack would show up. Then . . .

The man ahead of him grumbled, "He's like a ghost, damn him. You think you've got him and the bastard gets away."

Ross heard hoofbeats approaching along the street from the left. Sinking his spurs, he whirled away.

Immediately their shouts raised behind him. He heard the man who had spoken to him say in an outraged voice, "Why, the son-of-a-bitch! It was him all the time!"

He had a lead of about half a block. He headed toward the edge of town along the shortest way.

More shouts behind, more shots. More men gathered, it seemed from everywhere, and most of them had horses now. There was a steady thunder of hoofbeats in the street behind him.

He left the town, swung savagely to the right, and plunged his horse into the river. The horse scrambled, dripping, out on the other side, and Ross spurred him away into the darkness.

There was a little time for reflection now. And time to feel his utter weariness. He couldn't go on this way. Sooner or later he would exhaust himself and they'd capture him.

He rode at top speed for about two miles. The sound of the pursuit faded as they fell uncertainly behind. He heard a shout, "Stop your goddam' horses. Listen for him."

Almost immediately there was silence behind. Ross hauled in his horse and proceeded at a walk. He continued this way for nearly a mile, then abruptly changed direction. He heard another shout, and nothing after that.

A dozen posses would be out looking for him as soon as it got light because Judge Milburn had taken the pursuit out of Juan Mascarenas's hands when he posted that reward. It had become a treasure hunt.

But for the moment he was clear. His horse was not too tired. He could travel a long way before daylight came.

Far enough to get out of the county, he thought. They didn't expect that of him. He hadn't tried to leave so far, and now they didn't think he would. He could ride out to Horseshoe and get Lily Caine. They could leave the county together. He could forget all that had happened here.

There was an ache in his chest as he considered it. He turned his horse toward Horseshoe almost automatically.

What if he didn't stay and clear himself, he thought angrily. What possible difference did it make? Why should he worry about what these people thought of him, these people who would hunt him down like a wolf just because there was a large amount of money in it for them?

Phil . . . he had thought Phil was his friend. Milburn . . . Milburn had defended him. Mascarenas was sworn to uphold the law but he had also appointed himself as Ross Logan's judge. Ross cursed disgustedly.

Only Lily and maybe Sadie Plue of all the people in the county were willing to help him when he needed help. Neither of them cared what he had done. And his father . . .

He guessed he couldn't leave. He couldn't run now after going through this much. But he didn't change his course. Weary all the way to his bones, he needed tonight what Lily could give to him. Her belief. Her encouragement. Her love.

Foolish perhaps to go where they would reasonably expect him to go. Foolish to waste time that might be spent putting miles between himself and the pursuit. But a man can only do so much. And Ross was near the limit of his strength.

A hot meal. A chance to hold her close to him. The sight of her face, of her eyes resting so hungrily on him.

It was worth the risk. It was worth it to Ross who had, for fifteen years, known only bleak prison walls, the guards' brutality, the cold and womanless existence there.

After he had seen Lily, perhaps he would leave Vail and the valley of the Horseshoe for a while. Until things calmed down.

Give Phil a chance to worry. Let him wonder where Ross was, how soon he would be coming back. Because he would know for sure that Ross was coming back.

Let him worry and then when Ross finally did come back, he might be ready to talk.

Ross rode steadily through the night. He doubted now if they'd spend much time uselessly combing the plain. They'd probably return to town, search it thoroughly, then outfit themselves for the continued pursuit tomorrow.

Horseshoe. It had once been home to him. It could be home again. If he stayed and fought. If he did not give up.

A lamp was burning in the kitchen as he rode in. He exercised the same caution he had before, inspecting the barn before approaching the house.

Lily heard him and came to the door. She stood framed in its light, slender, startled, until he called, "It's all right, Lily. It's me."

She left the doorway then and came running across the yard. She threw herself into his arms.

And he held her now, tightly, hungrily, almost desperately.

Perhaps this was wrong, he thought. And perhaps it was not. But he was only a man and he needed her.

She pulled away and took his hand. Silently she led him toward the house.

The house that held his memories of Ruth, her memories of Caine. He said "No," and pulled her toward the barn.

The loft was fragrant, holding the smell of hay, a faint smell of dust. At the top of the ladder he caught her hungrily in his arms again.

They were not children, either of them. Both had known love before. But not this kind of love. Not this soaring breathlessness that seemed the fulfilment of a lifetime of waiting and longing and wordless yearning. In this moment there was selflessness and the desire to give. And out of that came an almost unbearable fulfilment new to Ross's experience and to Lily's too.

Afterward they lay sleepily in each other's arms and stared at the stars through the open loft door.

Lily's concern for him broke the spell. "Did you find out anything in town?"

He said softly, "Nothing tangible. Do you know that I love you very much?"

"I know. What will you do now?"

His weariness brought bitterness to his voice. "Keep running, I suppose. Keep trying."

For a moment she was silent. Then she said hesitantly, "I caught up two fresh horses after you left. They're in the corral. We could . . . we could be a long way from here by the time daylight comes."

The prospect was tempting, but he didn't consider it long. He knew no man can live forever on the run. Sooner or later someone would show up wherever he had settled. He'd have to stand trial, with conviction a virtual certainty.

Going back to prison would be unbearable, he thought. Leaving Lily under those circumstances would be much worse than leaving her to-night. Because if he left to-night, there would still be a chance for him.

He got up abruptly, pulling her to her feet beside him. There seemed to be new strength in him, a new determination to go on. He said, "Have you got anything to eat in there? Something that won't take long?"

"Some stew. All I'd have to do would be to heat it up."

He climbed down the ladder and helped her down after him. Both were strangely silent as they walked toward the house. Just short of the door, he stopped, pulled her close to him and kissed her gently. He said, "I've stayed clear of them for several days. I'll stay clear for several more. You're not to worry. Understand?"

They went in and Ross built up the fire for her. While he waited, he returned to the door and stared out into the night, listening. Lily began to pack another sack of supplies for him.

He heard nothing — just the sound of the breeze sighing softly past the eaves. Just the sounds of the two horses moving around the corral, and that of his own horse, shifting restlessly where he was tied.

Ross's eyes felt as though he hadn't slept for a week. But soon, perhaps . . .

Lily said, "It's ready, Ross."

He turned and sat down at the table. He could feel her eyes resting on him as he ate. Occasionally, passing him, she would reach out and touch his hair, or the growth of whiskers on his cheeks.

More than anything he wanted to stay

with Lily. Doing all the everyday things that other men did. He wondered if most men thought about it . . . how lucky they were. To do a day's hard work and at day's end to eat, and rest and to rise again the next day and do the same things all over again.

To be free, to enjoy the dawn, and the heat of the sun, and the coolness of the breeze at night.

He rose abruptly. "I'm always leaving, it seems."

"Isn't there *anything* I can do to help?"

"What do you think you've been doing? How do you think I'd have kept going without your help?"

"But I'd like to do more. I . . ." A slow flush crept into her face.

He grinned at her embarrassment and hugged her affectionately. Then he went out and crossed the yard to the corral. In spite of his weariness, he felt strong and alive. Lily had done that for him. And she wanted to do more.

He caught one of the fresh horses and changed his saddle and bridle to him. He led him back to the house, took the sack of supplies she handed him and tied it on behind.

He kissed her and mounted. He wanted

to stay, but some uneasiness told him he had already stayed too long. He reined away, lifting his horse immediately to a gallop.

If he had not he might have heard the sounds of approaching hoofbeats from the direction of town. As it was, he had gone nearly a mile before he heard the shots behind.

Chapter Sixteen

Ross Logan hauled his horse to a plunging halt, listening intently. Shots could only mean that men had arrived from town looking for him. But why should there be shots? Only Lily was there at Horseshoe.

Unhesitatingly he reined his horse around. If the damn' trigger-happy fools had hurt Lily . . .

The shots continued as he rode. She must be all right, he thought, or they would have stopped. But why . . . ?

The sky was greying faintly in the east as he brought the buildings at Horseshoe into sight. He halted his horse instantly, frowning.

Flashes from the kitchen window of the house . . . a moment later from a window in the living-room . . .

Flashes from the barn, the corral, from behind a tree in the centre of the yard . . .

Despite his concern for her safety, Ross had to grin. There was a woman! To give him time, to hold his pursuers here, she was making it look as though both of them were shooting.

His first and most pressing inclination was to ride on down there, yell and shoot at them, and so draw them away from the house. Then he thought of Lily, picturing her in his mind.

A woman a man could be proud of. He understood what she meant to do. She'd hold them here until sunup, giving him time to get a four- or five-mile start. Then she'd step outside, give up and let them search the house.

They wouldn't hurt her intentionally. And he was damned if he was going to let her efforts be wasted. She wanted him to have a start.

But there was both reluctance and worry in him as he reined away. She could get hit in that exchange down there. She could be hurt.

The light in the east increased gradually as he rode. The sky turned blue, then pink, then blue again. Once he stopped and listened intently, but heard nothing.

It was over back there by now. They had undoubtedly left Horseshoe and had picked up his trail.

He lined his horse out on a course that

led directly south, intending to get clear out of the county if he could. Long enough to rest up. Long enough to let the hue and cry die down.

He crossed the boundary separating Horseshoe from Vail's land. He had covered no more than half a dozen miles before he was forced to stop.

A dozen or more mounted men were approaching him from the south. They had appeared from behind a knoll less than a mile away.

He looked around frantically for cover. There was none. Right here the plain was completely flat, unscarred even by a wash.

They'd seen him anyway. Their horses surged into fast motion. A gun discharged exuberantly into the air.

Vail's crew, he supposed. Maybe even the ones who had been pursuing him yesterday. Now he had no choice. He couldn't leave the county. He'd be lucky just to stay ahead of them.

He turned and spurred his horse to a hard run. He headed west towards the badlands, for only in the badlands could he even hope to get away.

Glancing to his right, he saw a rising dust cloud in the direction of Horseshoe. That would be the bunch Lily had pinned down temporarily for him. Probably Phil Rivers and Sadie Plue's five sons.

He was between two fires. And ahead, somewhere in the badlands, was Juan Mascarenas.

Juan would be mounted. Probably rested too. He'd probably spent the night, or part of it, at Sadie Plue's.

An irritable anger stirred suddenly in Ross. He was tired of being chased, tired of being fair game for anyone who had a gun. He was tired of being falsely accused.

He was close to the point of making a stand. He was closer than he thought to the point where exhaustion would make it impossible for him to go on.

Thank God for the fresh horse Lily had given him. The animal ran smoothly, tirelessly, and slowly Ross began to draw away from Vail's men. The others, who had come from Horseshoe, came into the trail behind Vail's crew and, after more than an hour, overtook them. Looking back from a high knoll, Ross saw them riding in a group, spread out, probably wrangling over who had the best right to the reward.

That damned reward . . . that was something else Orv Milburn had to answer for. Because it had never been a reward in the strictest sense of the word. It was a bounty.

It was a fee for legalised murder.

But nobody had collected it yet, and maybe no one would. Maybe the bunch back there would get to wrangling.

The badlands loomed plainly ahead of him. Another five miles and he'd be in the midst of them. Once into them, his pursuers would have to resort to following trail because they wouldn't be able to see him any more.

How would they react to such a situation, he wondered. Would they continue in a group, sticking to his trail? He doubted that. There must be close to twenty men in the group. That many travelling the narrow trails in the badlands would get nowhere.

No. They'd split up, race ahead, and try to intercept him. With a fair chance of success, he admitted ruefully. The trouble with the badlands was that you couldn't see, at any time, more than a quarter mile ahead. If he stumbled onto a group of them . . .

Shrugging fatalistically, he put his running horse recklessly into a narrow, dry ravine. Without reducing speed, he raced along its narrow floor, avoiding rocks and an occasional clump of heavy brush.

To someone unfamiliar with them, the badlands were a maze. But Ross's fifteen years in prison had not destroyed his memory. He'd combed the badlands for cattle too many times in the past. He knew each draw, each towering eroded peak.

It was hot in there. The sun beat mercilessly down, reflecting from the canyon walls. No breeze dissipated or stirred the walled-in heat. Ross's horse began to sweat. Ross's own shirt grew dark.

He refused to admit it at first. He refused to believe that such a thing could happen to him. But after another mile, he had to admit it. He had no choice.

His horse was lame. What had been, at first, an almost unnoticeable limp, was now unmistakable. The horse was finished as far as Ross was concerned. He was afoot in the badlands, just as Juan Mascarenas had been a couple of days before.

He dismounted and picked up the horse's hoof. He examined it closely, for rocks, sticks, thorns. He found nothing. He examined the hock. It was swollen slightly.

Ross slid the rifle out of the saddle boot. He took the sack of provisions from behind the saddle. He began to walk, leaving the horse behind.

Soundlessly and bitterly he cursed the mischance that had made his horse go lame. He knew that, in leaving his horse, he abandoned his only chance of making an escape.

Alternately walking and trotting, he covered almost a mile before he heard shouts and shots behind, signifying that they had found the abandoned horse. They'd gather now. They'd talk it over and then they'd spread out and encircle him. Once that was done, all that remained for them was to close in slowly. Trap him in the centre of the circle and shoot him down.

But he'd pick the spot where they'd finally corner him, he thought. He'd find some high knoll where he could make a stand. There was still a chance that numerous and continuing gunshots would draw Juan Mascarenas to the spot.

He grinned to himself at his own inconsistency. He'd promised himself that he wouldn't be taken alive. Now he wanted Juan Mascarenas to intervene.

His reasoning was simple enough. Dead, no chance would remain to clear himself, no chance of seeing Lily Caine again. But alive, even if he was behind bars he could still try . . .

His lungs felt as though they were going to burst. He ran steadily, always along an uphill course, and always toward Sadie Plue's hardscrabble ranch. Not much chance of making it, but if he did, he'd be able to get a horse.

The silence of this place was complete. No sound from the pursuers now. No breath of air. No sounds of animals or birds. There was only the ragged, harsh sound of Ross's breathing, only the scuff of his boots against the dry hard ground and the occasional jingle of his spurs.

The feeling of being trapped brought a quiet panic to his heart. At any time now he could stumble into one horseman or a group of them. He could be shot from any high knoll.

He paused in the shade of a towering, red sandstone rock and drew great breaths of dry, hot air into his lungs. His shirt was soaked thoroughly with sweat. The sack and the rifle felt as though they weighed a hundred pounds.

But Sadie's place was close. Less than a mile away. And there was the faintest chance . . . if he travelled farther and faster than his pursuers expected it was possible that the circle might close behind him.

Thereafter he travelled on rocks, sometimes hopping from one to another in his effort to avoid leaving trail. And he succeeded, at least partially.

He was mildly surprised when he saw

Sadie's ranch buildings ahead of him. And jubilant. The circle *had* closed in behind him. They'd now waste the best part of an hour tightening it. He had a reprieve. He had an hour and a chance to get another horse.

But that hope faded as he rounded a huge pile of rock and saw Sadie Plue's corral. It was empty. For the first time in all Ross's memory, it contained not a single horse.

He stopped and carefully removed his boots. A lot of trails went in and out of Sadie's place. If he left no plain trail going in and if Sadie would hide him, by the time twenty excited men pounded in to Sadie's place and milled around there wouldn't be a decipherable trail left within half a mile of the place.

Ross realised grimly that he was grasping at straws. Why Sadie should hide him, he didn't know.

But he went on in, barefooted, carrying rifle, supplies and boots, and leaving hardly any trail. He went in and met Sadie standing in the door.

She was dressed to-day in men's clothes. She wore a battered, dusty, wide-brimmed hat under the crown of which her long grey hair had been stuffed. She was smoking a wheat-straw cigarette.

Ross gasped, "Horse went lame."

"Are they close?" Her voice was harsh and like a man's.

"Close enough." He expected her face to harden, expected her to tell him to move on.

Her face did harden, but she didn't tell him to move on. Instead she said, "Well, don't stand there. Come on inside. In a place with this many rooms and cubby-holes there ought to be someplace you can hide."

He went in, grateful for the shade and coolness of the place. He crossed the kitchen, got himself a dipper of alkali water out of the bucket and drank it greedily. Wiping his mouth, he turned.

He surprised an expression on her face that startled him. As she hustled him im-patiently through the house, he puzzled over it.

It had been the softest expression he had ever seen her wear. For an instant, for the briefest kind of moment, she had seemed like a woman to him.

She hustled him into a tiny room, piled high with supplies. There were blocks of stock salt, bags of sugar, beans, coffee. There were coils of wire and rope and against one wall a huge pile of soaked grain. She said, "Find yourself a place to lie down. I'll pile sacks over you."

Holding his revolver in his hand, he lay down among the sacks. Grunting with exertion, Sadie piled them in front of him, behind him, then crossed some over him. Walled in like this, he could scarcely breathe. But he kept wondering, and at last he asked, "Why, Sadie? Why . . . for me?"

Her reply was an irritable grunt. "Because you're Tom Logan's boy, that's why. And because I'm a damned old fool!"

She finished and went away, slamming the door almost angrily behind. After that, there was only silence in the house.

Because he was Tom Logan's boy . . . that expression she had worn . . . Why hell, Sadie Plue was in love with his father. Old as she was, tough and weatherbeaten as she was, she was still a woman and once, many years ago, she had been a girl.

Fifteen years before, Ross might have thought such a love ridiculous. He didn't now. Thinking of it, thinking of the softness that had been in Sadie's face, he felt a sudden tightness in his throat.

Two women . . . Lily Caine . . . Sadie Plue. As different as night and day. But both of them were women and both were capable of the highest kind of love — the kind that gives, and gives, with no expectation of return.

His eyes tried to close and his senses reeled. But he forced himself to stay awake. And waited, almost breathlessly, for sounds outside the house.

Chapter Seventeen

Time dragged. Ross lay still, sweating heavily from the heat and airlessness of the room. His body began to itch from dust and the scratchy material of the gunnysacks upon which he lay. His palm, holding the gun, was damp and slick.

There was no sound. Not for a long, long time. But at last he heard hoofbeats, growing in volume as they drew closer to the house

He tried to judge, from the sound, how many of them there were. It didn't sound like twenty men, but he could not be sure.

A new thought occurred to him. The Plues were almost as cagey on a trail as Juan Mascarenas was. His hopping from rock to rock and later removing his shoes might have fooled Vail's men but he doubted if it had fooled the Plues.

With Rivers, they had probably ridden here following Ross's trail and then deliberately obliterating it with their own.

He felt trapped, helpless. In the semi-darkness of his hiding place, he stared at the gun in his hand.

How could he shoot Sadie's sons after what she had done for him? And yet, how could he stand and fail to defend himself?

Voices now, shouting voices in the yard. The sounds of heavy footsteps within the house, reverberating through the floor. Talk. And more talk, the words of which Ross could not make out.

He heard the sound of the stove's lids as Sadie, or someone, built up the fire. He heard the sound of dishes as someone set the table.

And the talk went on.

He wished he could make out the words. He wished he could tell whether Sadie had succeeded in fooling them or not. If they'd followed his trail in why weren't they searching the house for him?

Maybe she'd convinced them that he wasn't here, that he'd gone on.

Or . . . and this thought was disquieting . . . they were just letting her believe she had them fooled. They must know Ross wouldn't be going anywhere just now. They might also want to be sure Vail's men were far enough away before they searched the house and captured him.

He felt like a mouse cornered by a cat, and the feeling angered him. He started to push the sacks away from over his head, started to get up.

Then he settled back resignedly. He couldn't precipitate a fight with Sadie's sons. Not on guesswork. Not after she had tried so hard to help him.

So he'd have to wait. Until they decided it was safe to search for him. Until they were sure Vail's crewmen were far enough away so that they wouldn't hear the shots and interfere.

Or until he was proven wrong in his guesswork. Until they rode away to comb the badlands for him once again.

He closed his eyes. He needed sleep desperately. He tried to remember when he had slept last. Two nights ago . . . Or was it three? He couldn't remember.

It wouldn't hurt to sleep right now. It would make the hours pass more quickly. If they began to search the house, the noise would awaken him. Or Sadie would, after they had gone.

Sleep came to him instantly. Once he began to snore and the sound woke him, and after that he was careful to sleep on his side so that the likelihood of his snoring again would be lessened.

Gradually the light in the room decreased. Its colour changed, from the warm light of daytime, to the greying light of dusk.

The cubbyhole in which Ross lay was completely dark long before the room was. But at last everything was black. And at last the air began to cool.

He wakened and stirred, grunting with the pain of his cramped position. His gun had fallen from his hand so he groped around until he found it again.

He listened intently. He could hear the soft murmur of voices from the direction of the kitchen.

He scowled. What the devil was going on? He couldn't believe that Phil Rivers and the Plues would give up the search for him like this. Not when they knew the badlands more thoroughly than anyone else.

Unless they knew he was in the house. But if they did, why had they waited so long?

And why, since it was now dark, could he not ease himself out of here, go through the window and escape?

He pushed the sacks carefully away from their position over him. One of them began to roll.

Raising up, he grabbed for it frantically.

His hands caught the rough material, but slipped away.

The sack rolled on, coming to rest against the wall with a gentle thump.

Gentle, perhaps. But a thump that could be heard throughout the house.

He got to his feet, stumbled because of cramps in his legs, recovered and reached the window. He peered out.

They knew he was here all right. One of them was stationed immediately outside the window. Ross could see the vague shape sitting comfortably on a nail keg about six feet to one side of the window. He could see the horses tied to a rail a little farther on.

And then he heard footsteps coming along the hall.

He backed into a corner and thumbed back the hammer of his gun. He waited.

They reached his door and opened it. Light from a lamp or lantern streamed in.

Luke Plue's voice came through the door. "Come on out, Ross. We know you're there. We wasn't sure which room she'd hid you in, but you gave yourself away."

Ross said, "Come get me, Luke."

Luke said harshly, "You got a choice, Ross. Come out, and we'll take you in alive. If we got to come after you, you'll be dead."

"So will you, Luke." Ross frowned lightly. Luke's voice was too persuasive, too soft. It roused his suspicions.

There was a slight scuffle in the hall. Another of Sadie's sons said, "Now, Ma, we ain't goin' to hurt him. Not if he gives hisself up."

Sadie's voice was furious. "Liar! To think I raised a pack of liars an' killers! I heard you an' Luke talkin'. You ain't goin' to take Ross alive. And you ain't going to split the reward with Phil! You . . . !" Sadie's voice was suddenly muffled as though a hand had been placed over her mouth. There were the sounds of another scuffle, and then Sadie's voice, still muffled but understandable, diminishing as she was dragged away along the hall, "Don't give up, Ross. They'll . . ." A door slammed and Sadie's voice faded into nothingness. A key turned in a lock.

Luke's voice again. "Don't pay no mind to her, Ross. She don't know what she's talkin' about." Its tone was wheedling. "Come on out now. You're worth a lot of money to us, more money than any of us ever seen."

Ross repeated softly, "Come get me,

Luke." He wondered if Phil Rivers was out there in the hall with them. Probably he was, and probably one of them had a gun in his back.

He grinned faintly as he thought of it. Phil was facing death. He knew, as Ross did, that Sadie's words had been true. Both he and Ross were going to turn up dead if the Plues had their way. They'd probably claim that they'd captured Ross and that Phil had tried to kill him. They'd claim either that Ross had shot Phil defending himself, or that one of them shot Rivers to prevent him from killing Ross. Only they'd been too late. Rivers had already fired, they'd say.

Nice and neat. And the whole five thousand would belong to the Plues. A thousand apiece.

The silence ran on, dragging heavily. Outside in the hall there was a whispered conference.

Ross knew they'd come in eventually. They weren't cowards. And they'd never had over two hundred dollars between them at one time in their entire lives.

There were five shells in Ross's gun. When the shooting started, there would be no time to re-load.

He eased toward the window. He

glanced out. The guard was standing up, facing the window now, a gun in his hand.

It wouldn't make much sense to try going out the window. He'd be silhouetted against the light filtering into the room through the open door. Even if he crashed through, the man outside would have one good shot at him.

Tension built in him intolerably. Any instant they'd come plunging into the room. He'd get one or two of them, of course. But there were four of the Plues in the hall. He'd never get them all before one of them got him.

He stepped closer to the door, placing himself directly behind it. Just as well make it difficult for them. This way, they'd have to come all the way into the room and whirl.

Out in the hall, the lamp suddenly went out. The room was in total darkness.

Ross plunged instantly toward the window. He heard their pounding footsteps as they spilled into the room.

Ross jumped, raising his knees as he did so that they were tight against his chest. He closed his eyes, briefly felt the resistance of window glass and frame, then was falling beyond. His ears were filled, both with the crash of glass and with the thunderous boom of guns discharging inside the room he had so recently left.

He struck the ground rolling. There was pain in his left shoulder, and a fiery burning which he assumed was caused by a glass cut.

The guard was shooting now. But wildly as though too shaken and surprised to take careful aim.

Still trying to bring his gun to bear, Ross continued to roll, momentum from his leap carrying him. Gunshots were an almost continuous thunder in his ears.

One, though, came neither from inside the house nor from the guard twenty feet away. It came from the other direction, from out across the yard.

Ross got to his feet and ran, glancing back over his shoulder toward the guard.

The man was down on his hands and knees. He was coughing, choking . . .

Ross reached the corner of a shed. He pulled up, out of breath, feeling the growing pain, the growing numbness in his shoulder and upper arm. Hell, that couldn't be a glass cut. A bullet must have hit him.

For several moments there was confusion at the house. Then the Plues began to stream into the yard. They found their brother who had been on guard outside the window. Luke yelled, "Ralphie, take him in to Ma. He's hurt bad. The rest of you, let's get that son-of-a-bitch."

Ross started to move out from the corner of the shed toward the corral. He stopped suddenly as a gun muzzle dug into his back.

The voice of Juan Mascarenas whispered, "Easy now. Easy. Gimme that gun."

Ross was silent momentarily. Then he said flatly, "To hell with you. There's still four Plues — or three even if they left one to guard Phil."

"Why should they be guarding Phil?"

"Because he knows they planned to kill both him and me and take the whole five thousand for themselves."

Ross turned his head, trying to see Juan's face in the darkness. He winced with the pain in his wounded arm. Mascarenas asked, "You hit?"

"I think so. Unless I got cut diving through that window."

"Bleedin' bad?"

"Bad enough. My whole sleeve's wet."

Luke Plue's voice roared, "Ralphie, bring a lantern when you come out! The rest of you take a look around the yard. He's got to be here someplace. I'll stay with the horses. He can't get far without a horse."

There was some grumbling at that, but Ross could see the vague shapes as they detached themselves from the shadow of the house and fanned out across the yard.

Mascarenas whispered, "Keep quiet. This way, mebbe we can take on one of 'em at a time."

He'd backed down on his demand that Ross surrender his gun, Ross thought. And that was a little surprising, in view of the way Ross had put him afoot in the badlands a couple of days before.

Ross said softly, "I never thought I'd be glad to see you. But I was."

"Don't be glad too soon. I'm still going to take you to jail."

"You don't really think we're going to get out of here, do you?"

"I've been in worse spots than this."

"Why don't you sing out and tell 'em that you're here?"

Mascarenas chuckled. "They wouldn't pay no mind even if I did. Let 'em find out for themselves. Let 'em find out the hard way."

Guns in their hands, side by side right now at least, Ross and the sheriff waited for one of the Plues to discover them. Because it was inevitable. It was only a matter of time.

Chapter Eighteen

Over at the house, the line of tied horses fidgeted nervously. Once Ross whispered, "You got a horse?"

"Yeah. Back there in the brush."

"Think we could get to him?"

"Mebbe. But I'd rather play out this hand. These goddam' Plues have been a burr under my saddle long enough."

"What if they kill Phil?"

"They'll hang for it."

Ross felt a stir of admiration for the man. Mascarenas was tough — as tough as they come. For the first time, Ross got the feeling that he was also fair, within the limitations of his own beliefs.

He said, "You won't believe this. But just in case one of us gets shot, Phil was the one that killed Ruth. He'd been seeing her behind my back. Maybe he tried to break it off, and maybe she threatened to tell me."

Mascarenas didn't reply. Ross said, "Orv Milburn killed Caine. Caine was black-

mailing him about the way he got Horseshoe Ranch."

"Got any proof?"

"No. No more than you've got against
me. But Milburn had a good reason for
killing him. A better reason than you say I
had."

Mascarenas was silent after that. Ross
held his breath, waiting. Soft, scuffing footsteps were approaching around the corner
of the shed. He took a forward step . . .

A blurred, dark shape suddenly appeared
at the corner of the shed. Ross said
sharply, "Freeze! Or I'll blow your goddam' head off."

The man leaped back, to be instantly
concealed by the shed. He bawled, "Luke!
Here he is!"

Mascarenas cursed softly. "Why didn't
you shoot him! He's interfering with a law
officer in the performance of . . ."

Ross interrupted, "He doesn't know
that. Besides, he's one of Sadie's sons."

"He'd kill you if he could."

"Maybe. If he tries I'll shoot him then."

Luke yelled, "Come on, all of you! Get
around that goddam' shed!"

There was no time for talk. The Plues,
four of them, came plunging in.

One appeared at each shed corner. Luke

and another brother came charging directly across the yard.

Ross fired at the one nearest him. He heard the man howl.

Splinters tore from a window jamb beside his head, stinging his face. Mascarenas's gun blasted methodically.

Out there in the middle of the yard a man went to his knees, skidded forward and fell on his face. He lay completely still.

Luke howled, "Stay behind that shed, both of you. Ralphie's hit!"

He stooped, seized his fallen brother and dragged him back toward the house. He dragged him in through the kitchen door, briefly illuminated by lamplight streaming out.

Ross was thinking that they must have left Phil Rivers without a guard. They *must* have. The one guarding the window had been hit earlier by Mascarenas. The other four had participated in the attack he and Juan had beaten back just now.

Maybe they'd slugged Phil. But almost as he was thinking it, Ross saw a figure burst from the kitchen door and disappear into the darkness of the yard.

A big man, one too bulky for Luke Plue who was lean, almost stringy.

They couldn't have slugged Phil, then.

Or if they had, they hadn't hit him hard enough to keep him down. That had been Phil who ran from the kitchen door just now.

He said shortly, "That was Phil," and added wryly, "He's worrying that the Plues will get me first and cut him out of the reward."

"You sound pretty bitter."

"Wouldn't you? I thought he was my friend. Now I find that he was carrying on with my wife, that he killed her and let me spend fifteen years in the pen for him. As if that wasn't enough, he wants to kill me now for a five thousand dollar reward. You think I ought to like the bastard?"

"I guess not. Not if all those things are true."

"They're true." There was no place either Ross or Mascarenas could go. They had to stay for now. If they went either right or left, they'd be shot by the Plue brothers waiting beyond each corner of the shed. If they cut across the yard, they'd be exposed to Phil's fire, and would be in the crossfire of the two on either side of the shed as well.

It was a stalemate, but it wouldn't last. Phil would precipitate something.

One thing was in their favour. The Plues and Phil were no longer working as a team.

208

Each was trying to get Ross before the other did, so that the reward would not have to be split.

Ross heard a soft curse around the sheriff's corner of the shed. He whirled . . .

Phil's bulky figure appeared there at almost the same instant. Phil's gun fired instantly.

Mascarenas grunted heavily and went to his knees. Ross swung his gun into line and fired. He fired a second time without waiting to see if his first bullet had scored.

Phil Rivers wheezed as the second slug took him squarely in the chest. He began to cough, bending double. He leaned against the shed to support himself. He raised his gun.

Ross stepped around the sheriff swiftly and kicked. The gun flew out of Phil's hand. The man was breathing heavily, hoarsely, and there was a strange, bubbling sound to his breathing as though his throat was clogged with blood. He put his back to the shed deliberately, then slid slowly down it until he was sitting on the ground.

Ross turned and knelt beside Mascarenas. "Where you hit?"

"Thigh, I think. It's numb. Straighten out my legs and feel 'em to see if he got the bone."

Ross did, then felt up along Mascarenas's leg. There was a wetness of blood about six or eight inches above the knee. His fingers dug deep until he could feel the bone. He said, "No. The bone's all right."

"Phil dead?"

"No. Not yet."

"Help me up."

Mascarenas leaned heavily on Ross as he struggled to his feet. Once, a sharp intake of breath revealed his pain. With a steadying hand against the shed wall, he approached Phil.

Speaking to Ross, he asked, "Where's he hit?"

"Chest. Got his lungs from the sound of it."

"Then he ain't going to make it." The sheriff stared down at Phil. "Can you hear me all right?"

Phil's head nodded ponderously.

"You're going to die. You got it in the lungs. Want to make a statement before you do?"

There was no reply from Phil. Mascarenas growled, "Ross says you killed his wife because she threatened to tell Ross what had been going on. Is that right?"

Phil's voice was harsh, hoarse. "How the hell do I know that what you say is true?

How do I know I'm going to die?"

"Cough once. Into your hand. Then look at what you've coughed up. Ever hear of a man making it with a bullet in his lungs? When he's got a hard three hour ride to the nearest sawbones?"

Phil held his hand to his mouth and coughed. He coughed as though he couldn't stop. Then he peered at the palm of his hand. It was dark, but the flecks of blood showed up against his skin. His voice, when it came, was thin and scared. "I don't want to die. Help me, Juan. Get me back to town."

"After you tell me what I want to know. You killed her, didn't you?"

"What if I did? The goddam' bitch . . . Hell, I wasn't the only one. But she didn't want to let me go. She wanted to be the one to break it off when she was good and ready to."

"What about Caine? You kill him too?"

"Why should I kill Caine? I hardly knew him."

"All right. You're a nice bastard, Phil. You let Ross spend fifteen years in jail for something you did. Then you try to kill him for a stinking reward."

"You said you'd help . . . You said you'd get me to the doc."

"And I will, too, if you last that long. We've got to get these damned Plue brothers off our backs first."

Luke came out of the house. He looked toward the shed and yelled, "Ralphie's dead."

Mascarenas shouted back. "More of you will be too, if you don't call it off. Tell these brothers of yours to come on into the house. Then you bring us a couple of horses."

"And if I do?"

"You might get off with thirty days."

Luke stood there uncertainly for a long time. Then he yelled, "What about Ross? We had him until you butted in. We sure as hell oughta be the ones that get the reward."

"Talk to Judge Milburn about it."

"You'll say we had him until you showed up?"

"I'll say that. Now call your brothers off."

Luke yelled at them and they shuffled past the shed corners and across the yard to the house. They went inside. Mascarenas called, "Horses. If you try anything, it'll be the last time you ever do."

"I wasn't going to do nothing. As long as you tell the judge how it was."

He came across the yard, leading two of

the horses that had been tied beside the house. When he was still fifteen feet away, Mascarenas said, "Drop the reins. Go on back to the house."

Luke did. The door of the house closed.

Mascarenas grunted, "Help me load Phil."

Ross walked to where Phil sat slumped against the shed. He knelt, then stood up again. "Phil's dead."

"Then help me up."

Ross hesitated. "Maybe I don't want to go back with you. How do I know I'll get a better shake than I did before?"

"I'm telling you. If you didn't kill your wife, then I'm open to doubt on whether you killed Caine. I arrested you for killing Ruth and I always believed you did it. Maybe I figure I owe you something for that fifteen years. Is that good enough for you?"

Ross nodded. It was the best he could expect. It was better than he'd dared hope for.

He boosted Mascarenas onto one of the horses. "What about your horse?"

"One of the Plues will find him to-morrow. He belongs to them anyhow."

Ross mounted the other horse. He stared down at Phil Rivers a moment, a lumped, anonymous shape in the shadow of the shed wall.

He felt no particular satisfaction at having killed the man, though he'd promised himself he would for fifteen years. He felt no particular hatred now for what Phil had done to him.

He found himself wishing this was over, wishing he didn't have to return to town.

He moved out slowly, following the sheriff's horse. Every now and then Mascarenas would grunt softly in the darkness, grunt with the pain the horse's motion caused. Once he turned his head and said, "You know, you saved my neck back there. Phil would've got me on his second shot."

Ross replied, "It wasn't intentional."

"Supposing it does turn out that the judge killed Caine. What will you do then? Stay here?"

Ross didn't immediately reply, because he didn't know. It would depend on what Lily wanted, he supposed. But he knew one thing. Lily was a part of his life. She would always be a part of his life.

He said, "First things first. I'm still accused of killing Caine."

He was thinking of his last session with Judge Milburn, thinking of the way Milburn had come apart. Orv Milburn was a rat but even a rat will fight if he's cornered and without hope of escape.

"When we get to town, we'll go see the judge."

"And he'll oblige us by admitting that he killed Caine? Guess again, Juan. It won't be that easy and you know it won't. He's not going to admit anything. In the end, it's going to be up to you. You're the sheriff. You've got to make up your mind which of us *you* think killed Caine. And then you're going to have to arrest the one you decide did it."

Mascarenas didn't reply to that. Hunched and silent he rode down the winding, two-track road leading through the badlands to the plain. The night air grew chill with the feel of coming dawn and at last, when they were less than two miles from town, the eastern sky showed a thin, faint line of grey.

Milburn would be asleep, thought Ross. He'd be groggy and maybe he could be bullied into admitting the murder of Caine. But he didn't really believe that Milburn could. And a nagging doubt touched his mind. What if he was wrong? What if Orv Milburn hadn't killed Caine after all?

He'd thought that when he proved he hadn't killed Ruth it would be over, and that he'd be free. Now he knew it wasn't going to be as easy and simple as that.

Chapter Nineteen

The town was silent as they entered it. Silent and sleeping as dawn crept quietly through the streets and sifted through the thick ceiling of cottonwood leaves over the residential streets.

Dogs marked their passage through the town, barking as they passed, barking long after they had gone on. The only other sound Ross heard was the metallic clang of a milk bucket as some early rising resident went out to milk his cow.

The judge's house loomed ahead, and Ross felt the tension rising in him intolerably. Everything depended on the next few minutes. Everything depended, not only on how he and Juan Mascarenas handled themselves, but upon the unpredictable actions of Milburn too.

They dismounted in front of Milburn's house. Ross walked to the porch steps, with Mascarenas limping painfully after him. Ross turned his head. "What do you want me to do?"

"Go on in. Kick the door down if necessary. Have it out with Orv. I'll be listening."

"You still think he'll admit anything?"

"Maybe not. But you say he's already admitted that Caine was blackmailing him and that he stole your ranch. If I hear him admit that, then I might be willing to go the rest of the way. I'll arrest him for killing Caine."

Ross nodded. He stepped up onto the porch and tried the door. He was surprised to find that it wasn't locked.

He went in, with Mascarenas following silently behind. He knew where Milburn's bedroom was, so he crossed to the stairs and climbed them quietly.

He heard Milburn snoring before he reached the room. He went in, not thinking of Mascarenas now. He crossed to the bedside and seized the judge's foot. He yanked savagely, enjoying this, and the judge slid off the bed and crashed against the floor.

Ross let him stumble to his feet and then hit him squarely in the mouth. Milburn staggered back across the room and brought up against the dresser with a crash. But he kept his feet.

Ross said angrily, "Want some more? Or do you want to tell me how you killed Caine?"

Milburn's face was slack, unshaven. His hair was tousled. A trickle of blood ran from one corner of his mouth. He licked his lips, then mumbled dazedly, "I didn't. I told you I didn't."

"But you stole Horseshoe. And Caine was blackmailing you."

"No. I . . ."

Ross crossed the room threateningly. Milburn glanced wildly around the room, as though looking for some avenue of escape.

Ross felt a strong self-disgust. He stopped in mid-swing as Milburn yelled frantically, "All right. So I did admit that. But you're not going to get me to admit I killed Caine. Not even if you beat me to death!"

"I might just try it though." Ross glared at him, his anger directed as much at himself as at Milburn.

He heard a sound behind him and swung his head. Mascarenas stood in the doorway looking at the judge. He said, "That's enough, Ross. I've heard enough to satisfy me. I'll throw him in jail and charge him with killing Caine. Then I'll see how much evidence I can dig up."

Ross felt as though a weight had been lifted from him. He was free. Free to return to Horseshoe . . . to Lily.

The sheriff said harshly, "Get dressed, Milburn. Get dressed and let's go."

Milburn stumbled across the room to the chair where he'd laid his clothes the night before. He put on his pants without taking his nightshirt off. He shrugged into his shirt and turned. "I . . . I don't want to go this way. I'd like to shave."

Mascarenas shrugged. "Go ahead."

They followed Milburn down the stairs. He went into the kitchen and built a fire in the stove. He pulled the teakettle forward so that the water would heat. He sat down, shivering, in a chair beside the stove.

When the water was warm, he poured some into a basin, carried it out on the porch and shaved. He went back upstairs, with Ross following, and got a necktie and a coat.

He was ready at last, looking as pompous and successful as he ever had. It was plain that his confidence had returned.

Ross knew the sheriff's case against him was shaky. He doubted if Juan could dig up enough to convict him. He said suddenly, "He's got an office up in front of the house. He'd probably keep whatever records he didn't want anyone to know about there instead of at his office down town."

"Might. Let's go see what we can find."

Milburn asked, "You've got a search warrant?"

Mascarenas grinned. "Nope. And you wouldn't issue one if I asked for it, would you? Not until you'd burned what you didn't want me to find. Come on, let's go."

Wildness showed briefly in Milburn's eyes. But he obeyed the sheriff's instructions and walked toward the front of the house.

There was a small iron safe in one corner of the room. Mascarenas said, "Open it."

Milburn crossed the room and knelt before the safe. His hand was shaking violently as he turned the knob. He moved the handle and the door swung open. He reached inside.

He whirled so fast he lost his balance and sat down on the floor. There was a Colt pocket pistol in his hand.

The hammer was thumbed back and the barrel wavered wildly. He laughed nervously but triumphantly. Looking at Ross, he said, "It didn't turn out the way you planned it after all. I'm going to kill you, Ross, and then I'm going to kill the sheriff with your gun. Or maybe I'll kill the sheriff first. Drop your gun, Ross. Then step away from it."

Milburn was trembling and scared, but at this range it was doubtful if he'd miss. Ross fumbled with the buckle of his cartridge belt.

He glanced around at Mascarenas's face. The sheriff wasn't scared. Or if he was it didn't show. But he obviously didn't intend to put up any resistance now. Perhaps when Milburn thought he had things going his way . . .

Ross's belt and gun thudded to the floor. He took a backward step.

Milburn said, "Oh no. You get clear back to the wall."

Ross retreated reluctantly. When Milburn picked up the gun . . .

The judge stooped, awkwardly, keeping the gun pointed at Ross. Ross hoped Mascarenas wouldn't try anything right now. He was dead if the sheriff did.

Mascarenas stood just inside the door, frozen. With his left hand, Milburn extracted Ross's gun from the holster and thumbed the hammer back.

A gun in each hand. He swung the muzzle of Ross's gun toward the sheriff at the door.

No matter what happened, Ross knew he couldn't let Milburn shoot. With Mascarenas dead there'd be no proof of what Phil had said before he died. Ross would be right back where he started from.

He didn't hesitate after that. He dived forward, letting his body fall, reaching for Milburn's legs.

A gun discharged thunderously over his head. A second gun discharged. He felt a bullet burn along his calf, but then he struck Milburn's legs with his shoulder and bowled him back.

He started to claw forward, to wrest the guns from Milburn, but stopped as he realised Milburn was inert, motionless. He swung his head and looked toward the door.

Mascarenas was holstering his gun. He grinned at Ross. "I knew you'd do that. But for a minute there, I thought you were going to do it too late."

He crossed to the safe and began pulling papers out. He scanned some of them briefly. "Letters. Records. There's sure to be enough here to see that you get Horseshoe back. Besides, I doubt if Milburn had any heirs."

"What about Caine's murder? He never did admit . . ."

Mascarenas stared at him steadily. "Then you weren't listening. I heard him admit it. As far as I'm concerned, the case is closed."

Ross grinned. Blood was oozing slowly out of the bullet burn on his calf. It had stiffened and dried on his left sleeve.

But he felt good. Better than he had for fifteen years. He could hardly wait to get out into the clean, fresh air, to feel the breeze blowing into his face, to feel the warm sun shining on his back.

Mascarenas had believed him guilty once. Now he believed him innocent. It balanced up. All debts were paid.

He left the stuffy room filled with acrid powdersmoke, and walked along the hall to the open front door. He stepped out into the cool, clean air of dawn.

He mounted, weary, but loose and relaxed for the first time in many days. He turned the horse in the direction of the ranch.

A woman was waiting at Horseshoe for him, a rare and wonderful woman. He cleared the limits of the town while still it slept, a faint smile touching his weathered, unshaven face.

His mind was remembering her — seeing her eyes, her mouth, her hair. His ears were hearing the melody of her voice. And his body ached for her softness and her warmth.

He touched his spurs to the horse's sides. His head was up as he hurried on toward home.